JESS THE BORDER COLLIE
The Arrival

Jenny looked at the pathetic little bundle her father was holding. It was so tiny Fraser could easily hold it in one hand. He had torn away the birth sac from the puppy's head but there was no sign that the little animal was breathing. Jenny held out her hand and touched a finger to the puppy's body. It was warm and she could feel his heart beating under his skin.

Then, as her father removed the rest of the sac, the puppy breathed.

'It's going to live!' she cried.

'Look, Jenny,' her father said.

For the first time, Jenny noticed what her father had already seen. The puppy's right front leg was twisted at an impossible angle. 'His leg!' she gasped. 'What happened to it?'

Also by Lucy Daniels

Jess the Border Collie 1: The Arrival
Jess the Border Collie 2: The Challenge
Jess the Border Collie 3: The Runaway

Animal Ark 1–32
Animal Ark Summer Special: Seal on the Shore
Animal Ark Summer Special: Ponies at the Point
Animal Ark Christmas Special: Sheepdog in
the Snow
Animal Ark Christmas Special: Kitten in the Cold
Animal Ark Christmas Special: Fox in the Frost

Animal Ark Pets 1–12
Animal Ark Pets Summer Special: Cat Crazy

JESS
THE BORDER COLLIE

THE ARRIVAL

LUCY DANIELS

**Hodder
Children's
Books**

a division of Hodder Headline plc

Special thanks to Helen Magee

Text copyright © 1998 Ben M. Baglio
Created by Ben M. Baglio, London W12 7QY
Illustrations copyright © 1998 Trevor Parkin

First published in Great Britain in 1998
by Hodder Children's Books

A Catalogue record for this book is available from the British Library

ISBN 0 340 70438 1

Typeset by Avon Dataset Ltd, Bidford-on-Avon, Warks

Printed and bound in Great Britain by
The Guernsey Press Co. Ltd., Vale, Guernsey, Channel Islands

Hodder Children's Books
A division of Hodder Headline plc
338 Euston Road
London NW1 3BH

1

'Come on, Nell,' Jenny whispered to the black-and-white sheepdog. 'You can do it.' She pushed her shoulder-length fair hair out of her eyes.

It was warm in the old stables though the weather outside in early January was still bitterly cold. It had been the coldest winter anybody around Graston could remember. The ground had been as hard as iron for weeks before the snow came. Now there was a deep covering of snow in the fields. Even the hardy Scottish Blackfaces that her father bred on his sheep farm were finding it impossible to graze. Fraser Miles, Jenny's father, had had to put out bales of hay for his flock of almost a thousand sheep in addition to their usual winter feed.

Jenny knew the extra expense of buying in the feed had been a drain on the farm's resources. But, right now, Jenny had other things to worry about. She and her father were keeping an anxious watch over the birth of Nell's puppies.

The Border collie looked up at Jenny with liquid brown eyes. Already three puppies lay snuggled into the sheepdog's side. Jenny looked at them and smiled. They looked so helpless with their eyes shut tight but they were already beginning to suckle.

'You're going to be great sheepdogs,' Jenny said softly to them. 'Just like your mum and dad.'

'I hope so,' Fraser Miles said, smiling at his daughter. 'I've got buyers lined up for them.'

'You never have any trouble selling Nell and Jake's puppies, Dad,' Jenny replied. 'They're the best working dogs in the Borders.'

Fraser Miles nodded. 'Good stock,' he answered. 'That's the secret. We've always had the best sheepdogs at Windy Hill.'

'And Windy Hill is the best sheep farm in the Borders too,' Jenny went on.

Mr Miles's eyes clouded and Jenny bit her lip and wished she hadn't said that. She knew her father was having trouble keeping the farm going. These puppies would bring in some welcome money. She didn't want to think about what would happen if he couldn't balance the books this year.

'Here comes the pup,' Mr Miles said suddenly.

Jenny watched, fascinated, as the next puppy was born. First the water bag containing the puppy appeared and started slowly to emerge.

As they watched, the puppy dropped on to the straw that lined Nell's whelping box. Nell immediately twisted round and began nuzzling at the birth sac, tearing the thin membranes away from the puppy's head.

Jenny waited anxiously as the newborn puppy raised its tiny head. Then the little animal snuffled as it took its very first breath.

'Well done, girl,' said Jenny, smiling.

Nell continued to lick at the membranes, uncovering the rest of the puppy's body.

'That stimulates the pup's blood flow,' her father told her. 'Let's just wait and make sure the pup is able to move. Then I think we can leave Nell alone. I reckon that's her last.'

The puppy wriggled slightly and lay still, a warm, wet little bundle with its eyes tightly shut. Then Nell lowered her head and began to nudge it towards her tummy. The puppy moved its head blindly and began to crawl. Jenny itched to help it but she knew better than that.

'Don't interfere so long as the pup is managing,' her father said, reading her thoughts.

Jenny grinned. 'It's so tempting to give them a hand,' she admitted.

Fraser shook his head. 'They have to learn to cope with life from an early age,' he explained seriously. 'Don't forget, these are working dogs, not pets.'

Jenny nodded and her hair fell over her face again. 'Oh, bother this hair,' she exclaimed, gathering it up and twisting it round her hand. She stuffed it down into the neck of her coat. 'I wish you'd let me get it cut.'

Her father shook his head. 'No, I think it suits you as it is,' he said shortly.

Jenny looked at her father and sighed. Mr Miles's eyes were on Nell and her puppies but Jenny could hear the pain in his voice. She knew that she reminded her father of her mother. People had always remarked on how like her mum Jenny was. Sheena Miles's hair had been shoulder-length too and exactly the same colour as her daughter's. Jenny thought that was why her father wouldn't let her get her hair cut, but she didn't dare ask him. He still missed her mother so much he got upset and even angry if he had to talk about her.

Sheena Miles had died in a riding accident the previous summer, when Jenny was ten. Jenny could remember the terrible pain on her father's face when Matt, her older brother, had haltingly told her about the accident. Fraser Miles hadn't been able to tell his daughter – he couldn't bring himself to say the words. He had looked the way Jenny had felt. It was as if the world had ended.

Jenny hadn't been able to cry – not at first. Not until her grandparents, her mother's mum and dad, had come home from Canada, and her grandmother had taken Jenny in her arms. She had cried then – she had cried as if she would never stop. Gran Elliot would talk to Jenny about her mother, and that had helped a lot. But then Gran and Grandad Elliot had gone back to Canada and Jenny had learned to cry quietly up in her own room. She had felt very lonely – and she still did.

She wished her father *would* talk about her mum. She sometimes thought of forcing him to talk about her. Her mother had often joked with Jenny about standing up to the men in the family. Jenny missed so much about her mother. She missed her affection and her understanding – but most of all she missed the sound of her laughter ringing through the house.

'I like it really,' she said in a small voice. 'My hair, I mean.'

Fraser Miles looked up. His hair was much darker than Jenny's. Both Fraser and Matt were tall and dark. Jenny was fair, like Sheena. 'I'd better get back to the sheep,' he said, changing the subject. 'I've still got a few more bales of feed to take up to the top field.'

Jenny nodded. 'The poor sheep,' she said. 'They aren't cosy and warm like Nell and her puppies.'

'Hill breeds like the Scottish Blackface have good thick coats,' Fraser reassured her. 'But even so, if this weather doesn't improve soon I think we might lose some of them. I had to haul seven of them out of snowdrifts last week.'

Jenny knew that in winter, sheep were always

in danger. They would turn their backs to the wind during a blizzard and could be quickly covered by the driving snow. She frowned. She knew Windy Hill couldn't afford to lose *any* sheep. 'Can't you bring any more of them into the shearing shed?' she asked.

'There's no more room,' said her father shortly. 'I've brought in the weakest of the pregnant ewes. The shearing shed doesn't give very much protection anyway. It isn't much more than a lean-to. What I really need is a new lambing barn.'

And lambing barns cost money, Jenny thought. The old lambing barn had been falling to bits for the last two years. It had finally had to be demolished after a particularly severe gale at the end of December.

'Will you be able to build one before the lambing?' Jenny asked.

Fraser shook his head. 'I'll need the money from the lambs to pay for the barn,' he said.

Jenny sighed. 'Lambing is such hard work – even in a barn,' she said sympathetically. 'If you've got to do it in the open fields it'll be even worse.'

'Don't you worry about that,' her father said, getting to his feet. 'The lambing isn't until spring and, besides, Borders farmers have been lambing

7

in the open fields for generations. I can manage one season!'

'Of course you can,' Jenny said. 'Nell and Jake will help. Nell will be back to her old self in a few weeks' time.'

'You've been a good help with her, Jenny,' Fraser said. 'Thanks, love.'

'Nell did all the work,' Jenny replied. 'I didn't have to do a thing.'

'Oh, yes you did,' her father said. 'You kept talking to her, soothing her, keeping her calm.' He smiled. 'You've a way with animals, Jen.'

Jenny blushed with pleasure. Her father didn't hand out compliments easily. He was a man of few words – but he was a good sheep farmer.

Windy Hill had been in Gran Elliot's family for generations. Gran and Grandad Elliot had given the farm to their only child, Sheena, when she'd married Fraser Miles. Then Gran and Grandad Elliot had emigrated to Canada, which was Grandad Elliot's home.

Fraser had been determined to live up to the trust Sheena and her parents had shown in him to take good care of Windy Hill. That determination had been even greater since Sheena's death.

'Can I stay and watch the puppies for a little

while?' Jenny asked. 'I'd like to be sure they're feeding all right.'

Fraser nodded. 'That would be a good idea,' he agreed. 'Just don't go getting too attached to them. You know they've got to be sold when they're eight weeks old.'

Jenny dropped her head and gazed at the four puppies. 'I'll try not to,' she promised. 'It just seems such a shame for Nell, not being able to keep even one of her puppies.'

'Nell's a working dog,' said Fraser. 'She's used to it – and by the time the puppies are ready to leave their mother, she'll be busy with the pregnant ewes. There's a lot of work to be done, rounding them up for their vaccinations before lambing.' He ruffled Jenny's hair. 'You're the one who can't get used to it.'

'Dad's right,' Jenny said softly to Nell as her father walked towards the barn door. 'I'd like to keep all of your puppies at Windy Hill, Nell.'

'Call me if there are any problems, Jen,' Fraser Miles said over his shoulder.

Jenny nodded. She bent again and laid a finger on the last little puppy. 'I wish I could have a puppy like you as a pet,' she said. But her father had told her often enough there was no room for pets on a working farm. Jenny couldn't help herself, though. It was her constant dream to have a puppy of her own.

Nell whimpered and Jenny looked sharply at her. The Border collie's eyes rolled and she began to strain, her flanks heaving. Jenny gasped, then she jumped to her feet and ran towards the barn door. The pale winter sun cast a watery light over the cobbles of the yard, reflecting in the frozen puddles.

'Dad!' Jenny yelled across the farmyard.

Fraser turned and, at the sight of her worried expression, began to stride back across the yard towards her. 'What is it?' he asked urgently. 'Nell's all right, isn't she?'

'I don't know,' Jenny replied anxiously. 'She seems distressed.'

Fraser followed Jenny into the stables and crouched down beside Nell. She was panting now, her flanks damp and hot.

Jenny watched as her father put a hand on Nell's side.

'There's another puppy on the way,' he said. 'But I was *sure* that there were only four. This one must be very small.'

'Is Nell going to be all right?' Jenny asked,

anxiously. 'She wasn't like this with the others. What's wrong, Dad?'

Fraser Miles's face was serious. 'She must be exhausted by now,' he said. 'Perhaps that's all it is.' He moved his hand to Nell's hindquarters, gently probing. 'There it is. It's coming out the wrong way round.'

'You mean not head first, like the others?' Jenny asked.

Fraser nodded. 'This one is a breech birth. That's hard on Nell after all the work she's already done.'

'What can we do?' Jenny asked. 'Poor Nell. Look, she's pushed the other puppies away.'

Nell arched her back and the puppies fell away from her. The collie's eyes rolled towards Jenny as her body twisted in pain.

'Hold her head, Jenny,' Fraser said. 'I'm going to give her a hand with this one.'

'Oh, be careful, Dad,' Jenny urged him. 'If the puppy is back to front you might hurt it.'

Fraser looked up briefly. 'Nell is more important than any puppy, Jenny,' he said shortly. 'And I'll do what I have too.'

Jenny turned back to Nell and cradled the collie's head in her hands. She knew how vital Nell was to the farm – an experienced sheepdog *was* more important than a puppy. If her father had to decide between them, she knew he would save Nell.

Jenny closed her eyes. Please don't let it come to that, she prayed. Please let them both be all right.

She didn't dare to watch. Nell looked up at her with mournful eyes as she struggled to give birth to this last puppy. 'There, girl,' Jenny whispered. 'Just a little longer. Be brave!'

Suddenly Nell's head dropped heavily in Jenny's arms and Jenny's heart turned over. 'Nell!' she cried desperately.

The collie turned her head and licked Jenny's hand. Her body shuddered, tensing – then went still.

Jenny felt the breath stop in her throat.

'It's OK now,' Fraser reassured her, scooping something up in his hands. 'It's over, old girl. Just you concentrate on your other four pups.'

Jenny's breath came back in a rush as she watched the sheepdog open her eyes and move slightly. She cast a quick glance at what her father was holding and when she looked back Nell was already licking her other puppies again, encouraging them to feed. The tiny bodies scrabbled blindly towards her but Jenny hardly saw them. Her father's words rang in her ears.

'What do you mean, Dad? The last puppy isn't dead, is it?'

Fraser looked down at her and his usually stern expression softened. 'No,' he said gently. 'He isn't dead. But he might as well be. He'll never make a working dog.'

Jenny looked at the pathetic little bundle her father was holding. It was so tiny Fraser could easily hold it in one hand. He had torn away the birth sac from the puppy's head but there was no sign that the little animal was breathing. Jenny held out her hand and touched a finger to the puppy's body. It was warm and she could feel his heart beating under his skin.

Then, as her father removed the rest of the sac, the puppy breathed.

'It's going to live!' she cried.

'Look, Jenny,' her father said.

For the first time, Jenny noticed what her father had already seen. The puppy's right front leg was twisted at an impossible angle. 'His leg!' she gasped. 'What happened to it?'

'It must have been growing like that for some time inside the womb,' Fraser explained, cutting the umbilical cord and drying the puppy with a piece of old towel.

'Oh, the poor little thing,' said Jenny, gently taking the puppy in her own hands. She laid him down beside his brothers and sisters. 'There,' she encouraged him. 'You feed too.'

But the puppy was far too weak. The bigger pups scrambled over him, pushing him out of the way. Even Nell pushed him away from her.

'What's wrong?' Jenny asked. 'Why is Nell rejecting him?'

'Instinct,' Fraser explained. 'She knows he won't survive. Look at him. He's so weak he can hardly breathe.'

'But he *is* breathing,' Jenny insisted. 'That must mean he wants to live.'

Fraser leaned over and laid his hand on the puppy's bad leg, testing it gently.

'I'd never be able to sell him,' he said. 'And you can't expect Mrs Grace to look after a puppy as well as us.'

Jenny bit her lip. Ellen Grace was a widowed neighbour of theirs. Fraser had asked her to come and do the housekeeping at Windy Hill now that Matt was at college and away all week. She was taking a winter holiday at the moment but was due to start in a month's time.

'She wouldn't have to look after him,' protested Jenny. '*I'd* keep him. I'd look after him.'

'You know the rules, Jenny,' Fraser Miles answered. 'Every animal on this farm has to earn its keep. This crippled little pup could never do that.'

Jenny blinked back tears. 'What are you going to do then?' she whispered.

Fraser looked at her in real concern. 'I'll have to put him down,' he said gently. 'It's the kindest thing for him. The other puppies will crowd him out. He won't get fed. He won't even get near his mother to keep warm. He'll get chilled, and that alone would kill him in a few hours. He'll die anyway. At least this way he won't be in pain. He won't suffer.'

Jenny looked at the puppy's poor crippled leg. 'Is he in pain now, do you think?' she asked.

Fraser shook his head. 'It's hard to tell,' he replied. 'Now be sensible, Jenny. You know it has to be done.'

Jenny swallowed hard. She knew what her father said was true. She had lived on a farm all her life. There was no room for unproductive animals on a farm. The little puppy moved in her hands and yawned. The tip of a tiny pink tongue licked her finger.

Jenny just couldn't let him go – not just yet. 'Can I have a little while to say goodbye?' she asked.

Fraser Miles bent over Nell. 'All right,' he said. 'I'll just wait with Nell to see she's OK after that last birth.'

'Thanks, Dad,' Jenny said. 'I'll take him into the house. It's warmer there and Nell doesn't want him here.'

She was almost at the door when her father called her. 'Remember what I said, Jenny. Don't get too attached. That puppy has to go.'

Jenny nodded and looked down at the puppy. She knew what her father said made sense. But it was too late. It was *far* too late for common sense. She had already fallen in love with this puppy.

2

Jenny carried the little puppy into the big farm kitchen, kicking off her wellingtons in the porch on her way. She laid him gently down on the rag rug in front of the Aga, took off her coat, then set to work sponging the puppy clean with warm water and drying him.

When she had finished she went to the dresser and pulled out a soft blue blanket. 'There, that's better isn't it?' she said to the puppy as she wrapped him up.

She gazed down at him. Now that he was clean and dry Jenny could see his markings properly for the first time. He was mainly black with four white socks. His muzzle and chest were white and he had black ears, the marking running like patches over both eyes.

'You're so beautiful,' she whispered. The puppy turned his head blindly towards her, nuzzling her finger. Jenny found she had a lump in her throat.

'I'm not your mum,' she said softly to him. 'I can't feed you.'

The puppy continued to search blindly. Jenny couldn't bear it. 'Maybe I'm *not* your mum,' she told him. 'But I can at least give you some milk.'

Swiftly, cradling the puppy in one hand, Jenny looked amongst the baby bottles they used for feeding newborn lambs. There were some especially small bottles that they used for the very tiny lambs. Sometimes a ewe would have premature triplets and those lambs were nearly as tiny as this little puppy. A ewe could only feed two lambs so one of her babies had to be hand-reared.

Jenny took down one of the smallest bottles, not much bigger than a dropper. Then she heated a little milk in a pan on the Aga. Laying the puppy down on the rug once more, she poured the milk into the bottle. She tested the temperature on the back of her hand.

'Just right,' she said, picking up the puppy in his blanket. Holding the little animal gently, she guided the teat of the bottle into his mouth. It took several tries but at last the puppy got a taste of milk and began to suck enthusiastically. Jenny watched him feeding. He might not be very strong but he was certainly full of courage.

'At least the other puppies can't push you away from this,' she reassured him. 'You didn't stand a chance against them. But don't worry, I know how you feel. Fiona McLay is like that at school. Bigger than me and always pushing me out of the way.'

'Hi, Jenny! What's that about Fiona McLay?' said a voice from the door.

Jenny looked up and smiled. 'Matt!' she cried. 'Nell's had her puppies!'

Her brother strode into the kitchen. Matt was eighteen and, last September, he had gone away to agricultural college. But he came home most weekends to help out at Windy Hill.

He ruffled his little sister's hair and looked quizzically at the bundle in her arms.

Jenny explained: 'Nell had four healthy puppies.

But this one has a twisted leg, and the other puppies were pushing him out of the way so he couldn't feed. I was telling him they're just like Fiona McLay.'

'What's she been doing to you?' Matt asked, running a gentle finger along the puppy's nose.

'Oh, just the usual,' Jenny shrugged. 'She's telling everybody Dad will have to sell up Windy Hill and her dad is going to buy us out.'

Matt looked up sharply. 'Is she?' he said. 'Well, Calum McLay *has* had his eye on Windy Hill for years. But don't worry, Dad won't sell if he can help it. And even if he does, he'll *never* sell to McLay.'

'So you think he *might* have to sell?' Jenny asked.

Matt looked suddenly serious. 'Things are a bit tight just now,' he said. 'But we'll pull through. We always have in the past. What else has Fiona McLay been saying to you?'

'She teases me about not having the right sort of jeans and stuff,' said Jenny. 'But that doesn't matter to me. I'm not going to ask Dad to waste money on fancy clothes.'

'Good for you,' Matt said approvingly. He frowned. 'This puppy doesn't look too good.'

Jenny let Matt see the puppy's twisted leg. 'Dad

says he'll have to put him down,' she said.

Matt shook his head as he looked at the puppy's leg. 'That leg *does* look bad,' he said.

'I want to keep him,' Jenny confided.

'You know what Dad says about pets,' cautioned Matt. 'And you'll be at school all day. Who would look after it?'

'It's a *he*,' said Jenny. She thought for a moment. 'I don't suppose Mrs Grace would want him around. Anyway there's no point. Dad is going to get rid of him.'

'You're not still worried about Mrs Grace coming to look after us, are you?' Matt asked.

Jenny's mouth set in a stubborn line. 'We've managed all right until now,' she said. 'I don't see why we can't go on as we are.'

'No, we haven't, Jen,' her brother replied. 'It's been a struggle – especially since I started college and haven't been around to help out during the week.' Matt smiled encouragingly at his sister. 'Don't upset things now, Jen . . . It was hard enough to persuade Dad to have an outsider around Mum's kitchen. You'll like Mrs Grace. It's for the best, really it is.'

Jenny didn't say anything. She had enjoyed helping Dad and Matt with the housework. Now it was all going to be spoiled. Mrs Grace was sure to want to do everything her way.

'Hey,' said Matt. 'Come on. Come outside. I've got something to show you.'

'What is it?' asked Jenny. But Matt was already out of the door.

Jenny shrugged on her anorak, picked up the puppy in his blanket and pushed her feet back into her wellingtons before following Matt out into the farmyard.

'It's a horse!' she said. Then, as she looked, she began to take in the state of the animal. Its coat was dirty and dull and there were bare patches on its back where the skin had been rubbed almost raw. Its eyes were sunken and Jenny could clearly see the outline of the animal's ribs. 'Oh, the poor thing,' she exclaimed, her heart going out to it.

Matt's mouth set in a stern line. 'Poor thing, right enough,' he said. 'Somebody has been treating him very badly. It looks as if he's been beaten. I couldn't find out exactly what had happened to him. I got him for next to nothing at the livestock market in Greybridge. It was lucky I happened to be there today. If I hadn't bought him he would have been sent to the abattoir to be put down.'

Matt's comments stung Jenny. She was glad her brother had saved this poor horse from the abattoir, but what about the little animal curled up fast asleep in her arms? Didn't he deserve the same care?

Jenny gazed at the horse. He was coal black and, even with his coat patchy and unkempt, Jenny could see that he must once have been magnificent. Scars had formed unevenly over old injuries but they couldn't hide the quality of the animal.

Jenny frowned. There was something very familiar about this horse. She put out a hand to touch his neck. The horse rolled his eyes nervously at her gesture. She drew her hand back as the big animal stamped and pawed the ground.

'Careful,' said Matt. 'He's wary of people. Small wonder when you imagine the kind of treatment he must have had. Poor Mercury.'

Jenny stood frozen in shock. 'Mercury!' she exclaimed, her memory flooding back. 'This is Mercury? *Mum's* horse?'

'That's right,' Matt replied. 'Didn't you recognise him? I don't blame you. He looks entirely different. Mum always took such good care of him. She would be heartbroken if she could see him now. I just *had* to rescue him, Jen.'

Jenny stood open-mouthed as Matt led the horse away across the farmyard towards the stables. Mercury! Her mother's horse. The horse that had thrown her! The horse that had killed her! How could Matt dare to bring that horse back here? What would her father say?

Jenny opened her mouth to warn Matt not to show this horse to her father. Her father would *never* keep him! He had sold Mercury immediately after the accident. But then Jenny recalled Matt's words. It was true, her mother had adored Mercury. What would *she* have done if Mercury had been in danger of being sent to the abattoir?

Fraser Miles came out of the barn as Matt passed with Mercury. Jenny watched as, at first, her father's reaction of frozen shock mirrored her own. He spoke briefly to Matt. But then, after a short hesitation, Fraser patted the horse, then set about assessing Mercury's damage, feeling his hocks, running his hands over the horse's flanks.

'Dad!' Jenny called, hurrying over to her father. 'You aren't going to keep him, are you? You sold him when . . . when . . .' she stopped at the sudden desolate look in her father's eyes.

'I sold him in a hurry,' her father replied gravely. 'I sent him to auction. I didn't even bother to find out who had bought him. Maybe it's partly my fault he's in this state now, poor beast. If I got hold of whoever did this to him I'd turn them over to the police.' Fraser Miles sighed deeply 'Once he's recovered, we'll make a decision about his future. Come on, Matt. Let's get some food into him. He looks half-starved.'

Jenny watched as her father and Matt slowly led the horse into the barn. She was torn between sympathy for the horse's mistreatment and shock that her father and Matt seemed willing to accept Mercury back at Windy Hill so easily. Why, after selling him, was her father taking him back?

But then, this wasn't just *any* animal, Jenny argued to herself. This was *Mercury*! And no matter how sorry she felt for him, she could *never* accept this horse at Windy Hill.

Suddenly Jenny felt very alone.

A small mewling sound caught her attention and she looked down. The puppy was curled in her arms, nestled in his blanket. Jenny gazed at him. A tear rolled down her cheek and landed on his nose. He stirred slightly but didn't wake up. Jenny cradled him closer. She wasn't alone. At least she had this puppy – if only for a little while. He was sleeping peacefully, his belly full. His life would be short but right now he was warm and happy.

'Dad says you have to die,' she whispered. A feeling of the unfairness of things swept over her once again. Then her head came up determinedly. 'Maybe you *do* have to die,' she said. 'But first I'm going to take you to my favourite place. I can't save you but I can give you a little more time.'

Jenny wrapped the blanket snugly round the sleeping puppy, unzipped her jacket and tucked the bundle securely into its fleecy folds. Then she set off for the place she always sought out when she felt unhappy – the keep.

'It's my very special place,' Jenny whispered to the sleeping puppy as she hurried out of the farmyard and up the frozen track to the hill beyond. 'And no matter what happens to you, I'll always have a memory of the two of us there.'

The wind lifted her hair as she crested the hill. Snow crunched under her boots. The wintry sun sparkled on the sea beyond the farm and gulls wheeled around the cliffs that marked the seaward boundary of Windy Hill. There was a rim of hard frost at the edge of the snow-covered fields and ice lay thick under overhanging hedges and fences. Blue shadows pooled at the foot of the drystone walls lining the farm track.

But Jenny didn't see any of this. Her eyes were fixed on a jagged stone structure perched on rising ground a mile away across the snowy landscape. That was where she was going – Darktarn Keep.

3

Jenny climbed the knoll to the ruined keep and sat in her favourite spot looking out towards the sea. From here she could see Windy Hill below her: the red roofs of the farm buildings bright against the snowy backdrop.

The farmhouse looked warm and snug, its grey stone weathered by years of sun and wind. The shearing shed stood at right angles to the house, its open side facing away from the prevailing winds; the small stable block made up the other side of the 'U' shape. The lambing barn had been tacked on to the end of the stables but it was gone now. Jenny sighed when she thought of the expense of replacing it.

In front of the farmhouse the fields stretched down to the cliffs and the sea. Down there, below the cliffs, was the fishing village of Cliffbay.

Jenny thought of Carrie Turner, a new girl at Graston School, who had moved to Cliffbay with her parents a month ago. At first Jenny had hoped they might be friends, but when Fiona McLay had overheard Jenny saying so, she'd laughed at her.

'Why would someone like Carrie Turner want to be friends with a boring little mouse like *you*?' she had said spitefully. 'Her mum is a famous artist – her parents are really well-off. My dad says their house must have cost a fortune. *And* they have a terrific boat.'

Fiona's jeering had upset Jenny, and discouraged her from attempting to make friends with Carrie. Maybe Fiona was right. Why would a bright and bubbly girl like Carrie want to be friends with Jenny? Carrie was outgoing and confident in a way that Jenny admired. She didn't think she could ever be like that. Not now that her mum wasn't there to support and encourage her.

Jenny often thought about her mum when she visited Darktarn Keep. Sheena Miles had always encouraged Jenny to speak her mind. 'Come on,' she would say when Matt teased Jenny. 'Are you going to let Matt get away with that? We girls have got to stand up for ourselves, Jenny!' Then Jenny would giggle and join in while her mother teased Matt in return.

Jenny smiled at the memory. It had been a long time since she had teased Matt. A lot of things had changed since her mother had died. Jenny knew Matt and her father loved her but they didn't seem to understand her the way her mum had. Jenny had grown even quieter since her mother's death early last summer, but Mr Miles hadn't noticed. For a long time he hadn't noticed anything very much.

Jenny couldn't help thinking that Carrie Turner would have handled her situation differently. Carrie would have had a good deal more to say about how unfair it was to get rid of Jess and to keep Mercury. When she was angry, Carrie's cheeks would flame as red as her hair and she never seemed to be at a loss for words. But Jenny hardly ever got worked up and when she did she always seemed to get tongue-tied.

The puppy moved in her arms, wriggling his small body into a more comfortable position. '*You're* my friend,' Jenny said to him. 'I wish I could keep you.' The puppy snuggled deeper into his blanket and Jenny lowered her face, feeling the warmth of him on her cheeks.

She looked down towards the farm. Her father was out in the top field now with Jake. The sheepdog moved like the wind along the edge of the flock, rounding them up, moving them into position at Fraser's command. The black faces of the sheep stood out against their white coats and the snowy surroundings.

Bales of hay hung from the winter feeding racks. She saw her father stoop at a drinking trough and raise his stick, bringing it down hard to break the ice that had formed on top. Jenny shivered. Even here, protected from the wind, the cold was beginning to bite her gloveless fingers. But the puppy, tucked in his blanket inside her anorak, was warm and snug.

'I bet you'd make the best sheepdog in the world if you didn't have a twisted leg,' Jenny said.

The puppy's nose twitched and his little pink tongue came out, licking her cold fingers, warming them. Settled in a corner of the old stone wall, Jenny watched the clouds that scudded across the sky. Out to sea the wind whipped the water into white horses.

Jenny loved this place. She spent hours here, remembering the stories her mother used to tell her about the keep in the olden days – stories about the Border reivers who had fought to protect their land and had run raiding parties across the border of Scotland and England to rustle sheep. Sheena had made the tales of the reivers come alive. Jenny's favourite character had been Jess of Beacon Brae, who had rustled more sheep than all the other reivers together.

According to legend, Jess had once sold an entire flock of stolen sheep back to his arch-enemy on the other side of the border. Another story told how he got his name. His leg had been broken in a skirmish with reivers from across the border. The rest of his party were killed, but Jess had escaped and climbed Beacon Brae, a hill near Graston, and lit a fire to alert the surrounding countryside to the danger to Graston's sheep. He walked with a limp for the rest of his life but he was a hero and ever afterwards he was known as Jess of Beacon Brae.

'Jess of Beacon Brae had a twisted leg too,' Jenny said to the sleeping puppy. She smiled. 'And he was brave like you.'

Jenny's gaze shifted towards the tarn, a small lake on the other side of a drystone wall below the keep. That was where Mercury had thrown her mother. She had died there, alone, because of that horse.

'I wish Mum was here now,' Jenny whispered to the puppy in her lap. 'Dad and Matt just don't understand.'

The puppy made a little mewling sound.

Maybe it was her imagination but she was sure he was looking better already. But when Jenny drew back the blanket and looked at his tiny twisted leg, she sighed. Her father was right. This little one would never make a working dog.

Jenny was lost in thought, her eyes closed, when she heard a voice and looked up. It was Matt, standing silhouetted against the sun.

'I thought I'd find you here,' he said. 'How's the pup?'

Jenny dropped her head. 'He's lovely,' she said. 'And he's feeding. But I know it's no good. Did Dad send you to get me?'

Her brother sat down beside her and reached out a hand, turning back the blanket. 'Dad was worried about you,' he said. 'He doesn't want you to get too attached.'

Jenny swallowed and a tear rolled down her cheek. 'I can't help it,' she whispered. 'He's so brave – and he's strong. You should have seen him drinking his milk.'

Matt ran a hand through his hair. 'You really love this little scrap, don't you?'

Jenny nodded, unable to speak.

'Dad can't afford to be sentimental about animals,' Matt said, looking unhappy.

Jenny didn't answer. She couldn't help thinking that Mercury had been saved but Jess wouldn't be. It was so unfair. She looked up at her brother. 'Do you want me to come now?'

Matt nodded. His dark blue eyes were full of sympathy. 'It's getting really cold now,' he told her. 'You'll freeze here.'

Jenny turned away, shivering suddenly. There was nothing Matt could do even if he wanted to. There was nothing anyone could do. She got up slowly. 'We're ready,' she said.

'We?' said Matt.

'Jess and me,' Jenny replied.

Matt's eyes opened wide. 'You've given him a name then?'

Jenny nodded. 'I called him after Jess of Beacon Brae. He had a bad leg too.'

Matt smiled. 'I remember Mum telling me that story when I was little.' He looked towards the tarn. 'You miss Mum a lot, don't you?'

Jenny wiped a hand across her eyes. 'She would understand how I feel about Jess,' she said.

Matt looked at her helplessly. 'Come on, Jen,' he said kindly. 'If it's got to be done, we'd better get it over with.'

Jenny got up slowly and followed Matt back down towards the farm. For all his sympathy, even Matt didn't understand.

Fraser Miles was just coming into the farmyard with Jake at his heels when Matt and Jenny arrived. Jenny reached down to stroke the sheepdog, running her cold fingers through his thick coat.

'You and Nell have a beautiful litter,' she whispered to him. 'And the littlest one is the most beautiful of all.'

Jake wagged his plumy tail and reared up, putting his front paws on her chest, nuzzling at Jess tucked inside Jenny's jacket. Jess stirred sleepily as Jake licked his tiny head.

'Down, Jake,' Fraser commanded and, at once, the sheepdog dropped to the ground.

'I've given Mercury a bran mash, and he seems to have settled OK in the barn,' Matt said to his father.

Mr Miles nodded gravely. 'I'll get the vet out to him as soon as possible.' He shook his head. 'I'll never understand how people can mistreat an animal like that.'

Jenny stared at her father, unable to speak. She couldn't ask him to get rid of the horse. But she still thought it was unfair to put Jess down and keep Mercury.

Fraser turned to Jenny. 'Did you have enough time to say goodbye?' he asked her.

Jenny nodded, holding back the words that filled her mind. She wanted to shout at her father – how could he keep the horse that killed Mum and not an innocent little puppy? But she didn't dare. She couldn't bear the thought of mentioning her mother's accident to him. She had *never* mentioned it to him. She didn't want to cause her father any more pain.

Matt glanced at her and pursed his lips. 'Wait a minute, Jen,' he said softly. He turned to his father.

'Jenny has really got attached to this puppy.'

Fraser Miles looked impatient. 'That's what I was afraid of,' he said shortly. 'If I'd just disposed of the pup straight away this wouldn't have happened.'

'No!' Jenny burst out. 'I'd rather have had a little time with Jess than no time at all.'

'Jess?' said her father.

'That's what she's called him,' Matt explained.

Fraser Miles closed his eyes in exasperation. 'So now it's got a name, has it?' he said. 'When will you ever understand, Jenny? I can't afford animals that can't earn their keep.'

'I know,' Jenny replied, resentment building up in her. 'But even a crippled puppy is entitled to have a name. You can't begrudge him that, Dad. It was only for a little while. Here – take him!'

She kissed Jess on the top of his head, hugging him gently, then with a whispered goodbye, held him out in his blanket to her father.

Fraser Miles didn't move.

'Aren't you going to take him?' Jenny asked brokenly. Her throat was clogged with tears and she was having difficulty holding them back.

Her father looked at her for a long moment.

JESS THE BORDER COLLIE

'You know, Dad, Mercury won't exactly earn his keep,' Matt said quietly.

Jenny saw her father go pale. A spasm of pain crossed his face. He drew a hand across his brow and closed his eyes. Fraser Miles was silent for a long time. At last, he looked over at Jenny and gave her a strained smile. 'Matt's right,' he said at last. 'If we can keep and feed Mercury we can surely afford to keep a puppy.'

For a moment Jenny couldn't believe her ears. 'Keep him?' she whispered. 'You mean you aren't going to put him down? He can be my puppy?'

Mr Miles grunted and turned away. 'That's what I said,' he told her. He turned back for a moment. 'But remember, Jenny, he's your responsibility. You'll have to look after him – and it won't be easy with him crippled the way he is.'

Jenny swallowed back her tears. Suddenly she was ablaze with happiness. 'Oh, yes, I know,' she said holding the puppy in the blue blanket close to her chest just in case her father changed his mind. 'I'll do everything for him,' she promised.

'See that you do,' said her father. He looked at his son. 'Come on, Matt, there's work to be done. I want to house some of the ewes from the bottom field in the far end of the stables.'

As Matt passed his sister he laid a hand on her shoulder. 'Happy now, Jen?' he asked.

Jenny beamed up at him, overjoyed. 'Thanks, Matt,' she said. 'Thanks for sticking up for us.'

Matt laughed. 'Us!' he repeated. 'I've a feeling it's always going to be "us" from now on.'

'Matt!' called his father. Jenny's brother hurried off.

Jenny looked down at her puppy. He slept on, oblivious to the fact that his life had just been spared.

'Us,' Jenny said. 'You and me, Jess – for ever!'

4

Jenny was sitting in the kitchen, still holding Jess in his blue blanket, when Matt returned from helping their father.

She looked down at her puppy. 'I hope I can look after him properly,' she said. 'It's all right for the other puppies: they have Nell. But poor Jess only has me.'

'I think you'll make a wonderful substitute mum,' Matt assured her, smiling. 'Come on, I'll give you a hand to get his bed sorted out.'

Jenny looked around the kitchen. 'A bed!' she said. 'I hadn't even thought about that yet. We don't have a dog basket.'

'A dog basket would be too big for him,' Matt told her. 'We'll find a nice cosy box and line it with newspaper for insulation. We can put that blanket in too for him to cuddle into. Jess looks as though he's really taken to that.' The puppy was snuggled deep in his blanket, eyes tightly shut, fast asleep.

Matt rummaged in the big pantry in the corner of the kitchen. He brought out a cardboard box. 'This will do,' he decided, setting it down near the Aga. 'You'll have to keep him in a warm place at first. Newborn puppies can get chilled very easily.'

Matt took a sheaf of newspaper and expertly lined the box. 'That should do,' he said.

Jenny laid Jess down in the box, tucking his blanket round him. 'It's perfect,' she said, standing up. 'But do you think he'll be warm enough? Won't he miss his mother?'

'You could put a hot-water bottle in beside him,' Matt advised her. 'Wrap an old jumper round it so that it's soft and furry – as much like his mother's body as possible. A ticking clock is a good

idea too. Jess will think it's his mother's heartbeat and it'll stop him feeling lonely.'

Jenny sorted out an old jumper and prepared a hot-water bottle, as Matt had suggested. 'What about feeding him?' she asked.

'Ah, well,' said Matt. 'That's going to be a little more difficult. If he was still with Nell he would feed whenever he was hungry. You're going to have your work cut out feeding him often enough.'

'I don't mind,' said Jenny firmly. 'I'll feed him as often as he wants. I could even sleep in the kitchen with him.'

Matt laughed. 'I don't think Dad would be too keen on that,' he said. 'But you're going to have to make sure your alarm clock is working. This little one will need feeding every four hours – and that means getting up in the middle of the night to do it. How do you feel about that?'

'No problem!' she declared. 'Jess is worth weeks of getting up in the middle of the night.'

'Let's see if you still think that when you have to get out of your warm bed when it's freezing!' Matt teased.

But Jenny *didn't* mind. She set her alarm clock

for four-hourly intervals and, when it went off, she slipped out of bed as quietly as she could, padding downstairs in slippers and a warm dressing-gown. She cradled Jess in her arms as she gave him his bottle, watching in delight as he sucked.

For the first two weeks the puppy went straight off to sleep after he'd fed, but gradually he was able to stay awake for a little while. The first time Jenny saw his eyes open was during one of the night-time feeds. He had nearly finished his milk when, quite gently, he opened his eyes, looked at her for a moment and then closed them again as he drifted into sleep. Jenny sat there holding him for a long time afterwards, too thrilled to want to leave him.

As the weeks went on, Jenny made time to play with Jess for a little while after his feed – until he grew tired and fell asleep in her arms. Her father came down one night and found both of them fast asleep, curled up in the armchair at the side of the Aga. He woke Jenny gently and sent her off to bed with instructions to turn her alarm clock off – he would do the next feed. Jenny agreed – after all, the sooner her father and Jess got to know each other, the better. But next day Fraser Miles was just as firm about the puppy as he pointed out that Jess had dirtied the floor, not the newspaper Jenny had laid out. Jenny went to clear it up. Maybe it would take Jess a *little* longer to win her father over completely.

'Mrs Grace is coming this morning,' Fraser Miles told Jenny when Jess was four weeks old. 'I hope you're going to make her welcome. She's looking forward to getting to know you properly.'

Jenny looked up from tidying Jess's box and yawned. She had been able to cut down on the middle of the night feeds as Jess grew bigger and stronger, but she was still tired. Right at this moment Jess was lapping up an egg whisked in milk.

'I *do* know her,' she replied. 'She always says hello when I see her in Graston.'

'This is a bit different,' her father said. 'After all, she's going to be round the house a lot.'

Jenny reached out a hand and stroked Jess's coat. The puppy's eyes had been open for two weeks now and he was even beginning to cut his first teeth. Soon he would be chewing everything in sight. What would Mrs Grace say about that?

Jess lifted his head from his bowl and sneezed,

looking surprised at the sound. He was learning to lap but sometimes he blew out into his milk and the bubbles tickled his nose.

'Whoops!' said Jenny. 'Lap, don't blow, Jess.'

'If you can get him on to solids you'll be able to cut down even more on the feeds,' Mr Miles said.

Jenny yawned again and nodded. 'Matt says I can try him with baby cereal or porridge, or a tiny bit of minced meat.'

Her father nodded. 'The more protein he gets the stronger his bones and muscles will grow,' he told her, coming over to have a look at Jess. 'You've done well, Jenny. Looking after such a young puppy is a lot of work.'

Jenny flushed with pleasure. 'I don't mind the work so long as Jess is well.'

Jess polished off the last of his egg and milk, and turned his head, looking for Jenny. He wobbled uncertainly on his three good legs. His right front leg was twisted to the side and the paw didn't reach the floor. He took a few steps towards Jenny before tumbling sideways. Jenny watched as Jess tried to struggle to his feet again but his twisted leg gave way under him.

'He can find his balance on just three legs if I

put him down on the floor,' Jenny explained. 'It's just that he finds it difficult to get up again if he falls over. He's trying his best though.'

Jenny picked Jess up gently and gave him a cuddle before laying him back in his box. Jess promptly closed his eyes and fell fast asleep.

'Learning to walk isn't easy for him,' Fraser said. 'You can't expect him to walk as soon as a normal puppy.'

Jenny nodded. She visited Nell and her litter every day but she was careful not to make pets of the other puppies. Jess's brothers and sisters were much bigger than he was and already starting to explore their surroundings.

'He'll catch up,' she said.

Fraser Miles ruffled her hair. 'If his determination is anything like yours, he certainly will. You've thought of nothing but that puppy for the last month.'

Jenny had spent all the time she could with the little dog, feeding him and looking after him. She even managed to dash home from school at lunchtime to feed him. But Jess would soon be getting out of his box by himself when Jenny wasn't there, and scrambling about the kitchen. He was sure to get in the housekeeper's way.

'Do you think Mrs Grace will mind Jess?' Jenny asked anxiously. 'Puppies can be a lot of trouble round the house. Maybe she won't like him.'

'I've told her about Jess,' her father said. 'She says she doesn't mind him in the kitchen.'

Jenny looked up, alarmed. 'Do you mean she won't let him run round the rest of the house – even when he's house-trained?' she asked.

Her father shrugged. 'You'll just have to wait and see,' he said. 'After all, Mrs Grace will be in charge of the house from now on.'

The sound of a car engine came from outside and Fraser looked round. 'That'll be her now,' he said. 'Be nice to her, Jenny. I'm not going to be around much to welcome her; I'm so busy on the farm. Some of the sheep need their feet trimmed, and I'm trying to get records up to date, ready for the lambing.'

Her father looked tired and strained. Foot-trimming was a hard job. It had to be done by hand, with clippers. If the horny outer surface of the sheep's foot wasn't trimmed it could make the animal lame.

Jenny also knew that until her death last year, her mother had done most of the record-keeping for the farm. This was the first year that her father was having to tackle it on his own.

'Oh, and I'm expecting Calum McLay some time today,' Fraser added, running a hand through his hair. 'If you see him before you go to school, tell him I'll be up in the top field.'

Jenny nodded, feeling rather alarmed. Calum McLay and her father had fallen out with each other years ago, before she was born. Mr McLay really seemed to hate her father and Fraser Miles avoided him whenever he could. Why had her father agreed to see Mr McLay today? Not about selling Windy Hill to him, surely! Matt had told her that their father would never sell to McLay!

'Anybody home?' called a voice at the open kitchen door.

Jenny took a deep breath. It was Mrs Grace. She cast a quick look round the kitchen, wondering what the housekeeper would think of it. She frowned as her eyes took in the dusty surface of the dresser and the dullness of the row of brass jelly moulds hanging from one of the wooden beams. Even the blue-checked curtains at the window looked as if they could do with a wash. A pile of newspapers, weeks old, was stacked by the back door.

Jenny bit her lip. The kitchen hadn't always been

untidy. When her mother had been alive the brass shone, the wooden surfaces gleamed and there were potted plants in the windows. She sighed. Everything at Windy Hill had been different since her mother died. And now here was Mrs Grace – and everything was going to change again.

5

Fraser Miles invited Mrs Grace into the kitchen. Jenny picked Jess up. The puppy yawned and nuzzled her finger. 'You've got to be good, Jess,' Jenny whispered. 'Best behaviour.'

'Hello, Jenny,' Mrs Grace said as she came into the kitchen. She smiled. 'This must be Jess.'

Jenny nodded. 'I've started to toilet-train him,' she blurted out. 'He won't be any trouble.'

Ellen Grace laughed and her eyes lit up. She wasn't very tall and her brown hair was soft and curly. Her blue eyes were the warm blue of a summer sky, not dark blue like Matt's and Fraser's.

Mrs Grace was a widow. Jenny couldn't remember her husband. He had died a long time ago, her dad had told her.

'I expect Jess'll have the odd accident for a while yet,' Mrs Grace said, her eyes twinkling. 'But I'm sure we can cope with that. I'll keep lots of newspaper handy just in case.' She looked at the pile of newspapers by the door. 'Those will be perfect. Do you put him on the newspaper just after his feeds?'

Jenny relaxed a little. Maybe things wouldn't be so bad after all. 'If you watch him you'll see that he whimpers a little and tries to turn in a circle. That usually means he's ready. Sometimes he sniffs the floor. But sometimes he forgets.'

'He's very young,' said Mrs Grace kindly. 'You can't expect him to get it right all the time. What about feeding him?'

'Oh, you don't have to feed him or anything,' Jenny assured the new housekeeper. 'I've started him on solids now. I feed him before I go to school and I come home at lunchtime to do his midday feed. The next one isn't due until four o'clock so I'll be home for that one too.'

'That's excellent,' Mrs Grace replied. 'After all, you know how he likes his food prepared. But I could watch how you do it and, any day you don't have time to come home at lunchtime, I can feed him. I'll need to talk to you about what you and your dad like to eat as well. There's no point in me giving you meals you won't enjoy.'

Jenny smiled. 'I'll make a list of all our favourite meals.'

'Wonderful,' said Mrs Grace. 'Now, why don't you and Jess take me on a tour of the house and show me where everything is?'

Jenny set Jess down on the floor. Immediately the puppy wobbled over to Mrs Grace, holding his twisted leg up. He began to sniff at her shoes.

'Oh, the poor thing,' said Mrs Grace. 'I didn't know he was injured. What happened?'

Jenny looked warily at the woman. Maybe she wouldn't have time for Jess now she knew he was crippled. 'He was born like that,' she said. 'But he's learning to manage on just three legs.'

Mrs Grace bent down and held out her hand. Jess put his little pink nose into it and licked her fingers. 'The poor little scrap!' she said. She looked up at Fraser Miles. 'What does Tom Palmer say?' she asked.

Fraser looked surprised. 'The vet?' he said. 'I haven't asked Tom to look at Jess.'

Ellen Grace didn't say anything. She just looked calmly at Jenny's father.

'I was going to ring Tom tomorrow to come and check up on Mercury,' Mr Miles said quickly. 'Maybe I can get him to have a look at the pup then.'

'I think that would be a very good idea,' Mrs Grace said firmly. She looked at Jenny. 'Maybe it would be best if you asked him to call on Saturday when Jenny is here.'

Jenny gazed at Mrs Grace. She hadn't felt able to ask her father to go to the expense of sending for the vet. But the new housekeeper had suggested it just like that!

'Well, I'll be getting on up to the top field then,' Fraser Miles said, looking slightly embarrassed. 'You can show Mrs Grace where everything is, Jenny.'

Jenny watched her father stride out of the kitchen. Through the window she could see Nell and Jake lying in the sun. The frost had all gone now and already there was warmth in the sun. Her father had taken the ewes out of the shearing shed and the stables and put them back in the fields to graze. Spring wasn't far away.

Mr Miles crossed the yard, gave a low whistle and got into the jeep. The sheepdogs sprang to their feet and leaped up into the back of the vehicle as it started up. Her father didn't even look round. He knew they'd be there. The two working dogs obeyed every command.

'You're not that obedient, are you, Jess?' Jenny giggled as Jess lolloped over to her and began trying to undo her shoelaces. 'One word from me and you do as you like.'

'Puppies are like that,' said Mrs Grace. 'But with training they learn.'

'Thank you for asking Dad to let the vet see Jess,' Jenny said shyly.

'I'm surprised it's taken so long,' said Mrs Grace, her face puzzled.

'Dad's been busy lately,' Jenny explained. 'I didn't like to bother him. And anyway . . .' she stopped.

'What?' asked Mrs Grace.

'Vets cost money,' Jenny finished.

Mrs Grace smiled comfortably. 'I'm sure it wasn't the money,' she said. 'You're probably right. Your father has just been too busy to think about it.'

'Do you think the vet could help Jess?' Jenny asked.

Mrs Grace shook her head. 'I don't know, Jenny,'

she replied. 'We'll just have to wait and see. But we can hope, can't we?'

Jenny looked at Jess, hobbling around on three legs, his twisted leg held up.

'Yes,' she said. 'We can hope.' It sounded nice, that 'we'. Maybe having Mrs Grace here wasn't such a bad idea after all.

Jenny was leaving for school when Calum McLay arrived. Mr McLay farmed the land adjoining Windy Hill. His farm was the biggest in the area and he never let anyone forget it. He drove up to the gate just as Jenny was closing it behind her. 'Where's your father?' he asked gruffly.

Jenny looked at him, sitting behind the wheel of his shiny new Land Rover. Mr McLay's dark hair was cut very short and right now he was looking even more bad-tempered than usual. 'He's gone up to the top field,' Jenny answered.

'What's he doing there?' McLay barked. 'I told him I was coming to see him.'

'He's foot-trimming,' said Jenny, trying to be polite.

'Well, I don't have time to go running all over the countryside trying to find him,' Mr McLay said. 'Tell him I'll up my offer if he's prepared ' see sense. He'd be a fool not to take it with Windy Hill in its present state.'

'What offer?' said Jenny, alarmed.

'My offer to buy Windy Hill,' snapped Calum McLay. He looked narrowly at her. 'So he hasn't told you about it, has he? Well, you know now. I want Windy Hill, and what I want, I get.'

With that, Calum McLay revved the engine and turned his Land Rover in the muddy track. Mud spurted from its wheels, splashing Jenny's skirt, but she barely noticed. An offer! She hadn't realised things had gone as far as that. She turned as Mrs Grace came across the farmyard and stood on the other side of the gate.

'I see my landlord has come calling,' she said easily. 'What did he want?'

'Your landlord?' asked Jenny.

Mrs Grace nodded. 'Calum McLay owns the cottage I rent,' she explained. 'I've been trying to get him to repair the roof for months but he just ignores me. I'm afraid Calum and I don't get on very well.'

'He and Dad don't get on either,' said Jenny absently. Mrs Grace put a hand on her shoulder. 'What is it, Jenny?' she asked.

Jenny looked at the housekeeper. 'Mr McLay

says he's made an offer to buy our farm,' she said. 'You don't think Dad's going to sell Windy Hill, do you?' she asked, anxiously.

Mrs Grace pursed her lips. 'No, I don't, Jenny,' she said firmly. 'But if you're worried about it you should speak to your father.'

Jenny nodded. 'I'll do that,' she said. 'Thanks, Mrs Grace.'

Jenny couldn't get Mr McLay's visit out of her mind. It worried her all morning.

Carrie Turner noticed. 'What's wrong, Jenny?' she asked at mid-morning break. Jenny had hardly spoken to Carrie before but Carrie looked so sympathetic she couldn't help telling her what was worrying her.

Carrie pushed her bright red hair back from her face, her blue eyes sparkling fierily. 'Well, of all the cheek,' she said. 'Mr McLay must think he can do whatever he likes just because he's got plenty of money. I reckon Mrs Grace is right. You ask your dad about it, Jenny. Don't take Mr McLay's word for it.'

'It's true that Windy Hill is short of money,' Jenny confided. 'Maybe Dad *can't* afford to keep it going.'

'Don't you think he would have told you if he was going to sell it?' asked Carrie.

'Maybe,' answered Jenny. 'But maybe he didn't want to worry me.'

Carrie put her hands on her hips. 'My mum says there's no point in meeting trouble halfway,' she announced. 'Worrying doesn't solve anything. If he *is* thinking of selling, *then* you can worry, but not before you find out the truth.'

Jenny smiled. Carrie was so positive. 'How can I stop worrying?' she asked.

'Oh, that's easy,' said Carrie breezily. 'It's geography next. You can help me with my project. It's a complete mess. It needs somebody to tidy it up and sort it out.'

Jenny burst out laughing. 'You think that'll take my mind off things?' she said.

Carrie shook her head. 'Just you wait till you see my project,' she said darkly. 'It's *monumentally* awful.'

The bell went for end of break and Carrie took Jenny by the arm, leading her towards their classroom. 'Where is Paraguay anyway?'

'Calum McLay had no right to speak to you about it,' Fraser Miles said at lunchtime.

Jenny had cycled home from school in double-quick time. Now she was sitting on the floor with Jess on her lap. The puppy had eaten every scrap of the porridge Jenny had prepared for him.

'But is it true, Dad?' she asked.

Fraser Miles looked at her sternly. 'It's true he's made me an offer for the farm,' he replied. 'A very good offer.' Jenny's heart sank.

Then her father started to speak again. 'But there's no way I'll ever sell Windy Hill and certainly not to him. You can stop worrying, Jenny. Windy Hill belongs to this family – and it always will.'

Jenny buried her face in Jess's soft fur and the little puppy wagged his stumpy tail and licked her face.

'There now,' said Mrs Grace comfortably. 'You've had a morning's worry for nothing, Jenny.'

Jenny looked up and smiled. 'Half a morning,' she said. 'I spent the other half sorting out Carrie Turner's geography project.'

'That was kind of you,' Mrs Grace complimented her.

Jenny put her head on one side. 'Actually, it was kind of Carrie. She was really nice to me.'

'Why don't you ask her to tea?' Mrs Grace suggested.

Jenny looked up, surprised. She hadn't had anybody to tea since her mother had died. That was one of the things that had changed at Windy Hill. Her mother had liked her to have friends for tea. Mr Miles never seemed to think about it.

'Maybe I will,' Jenny said. She kissed Jess on the nose. 'You'd like to meet Carrie, wouldn't you, Jess?' she asked.

Jess snuffled and sneezed. 'I'll take that as a "yes",' Jenny told him, laughing. 'Now, don't you go catching cold or Mr Palmer will have to give you medicine. He's coming to see you on Saturday.'

Jenny could hardly wait for Mr Palmer's visit. The vet first examined Mercury out in the yard, and seemed pleased with his progress.

'He's a lot better,' the big, red-faced man pronounced.

Jenny stood well back, in the kitchen doorway, while Tom Palmer completed his examination. Jenny's mum had taught both her and Matt to ride when they were young, and Jenny was usually perfectly at ease around horses. Indeed, she remembered being perfectly at ease around Mercury – until last summer, when he'd caused her mother's death. Now things were different, and Jenny was very nervous of him.

Mercury was recovering well. He was putting on weight; his ribs didn't show through his skin any longer, and his coat was growing back thick and glossy.

'He'll always have a few scars,' Tom Palmer said. 'He must have had some rough treatment. But good feeding and grooming should take care of the rest of his troubles.' The vet looked round, his face serious. 'Have you found out who did this to him yet, Fraser?'

Fraser Miles nodded. 'I made inquiries,' he said. 'I've handed the name of his previous owner over to the police and I've informed the RSPCA. It seems Mercury was a bit too much for him to handle so he resorted to ill-treatment to try and tame him. I don't think it'll be easy for him to talk his way out of a prosecution.'

'Good for you,' Tom Palmer boomed approvingly. 'Animals are just like people. They respond to kindness, not cruelty.'

Jenny really liked Mr Palmer. He was always cheerful but she wondered if he was a bit noisy for Jess. Maybe he would frighten the puppy. But Mercury didn't seem to mind Tom's booming voice and the horse was usually very skittish.

'How would you like to ride Mercury one day?' Tom Palmer called to Jenny. She shrank back instinctively, shaking her head. She still couldn't bring herself to go near Mercury. She didn't like to see any animal in pain but she couldn't *like* him. Not after what he'd done to her mother.

'He's a bit frisky for Jenny,' Matt said. 'Maybe once he's been here a while and calms down she'll change her mind.'

'No,' said Fraser Miles shortly. 'You can exercise Mercury if you're careful, Matt, but I don't want to see Jenny up on him.'

Jenny looked gratefully at her father. He might have taken Mercury in, but it was clear that he didn't think the big horse was safe for her.

'I guess you're right, Dad,' Matt said. 'I've got a lot more experience as a rider than Jenny.'

Jenny frowned. Her mother had been an excellent rider and look what Mercury had done to her. 'You *will* be careful, Matt, won't you?' she said.

Matt ruffled her hair. 'Don't you worry, Jen,' he reassured her. 'I won't take him out until I'm sure he's recovered.'

Jenny frowned again. That wasn't what she had meant. It was *Matt* she was worried about, not

Mercury. But, looking at the way Matt was stroking Mercury, Jenny could see that her brother wouldn't listen to any criticism of the horse. He had rescued the animal and all he could think about was Mercury's wellbeing.

Tom gave Mercury a slap on the rump and the big horse danced, hooves clattering on the cobbled yard. Jess wriggled in Jenny's arms but she kept a firm hold on him. She didn't want Jess going anywhere near those big, dangerous hoofs.

'Let's have a look at this little fellow then,' Tom Palmer boomed, striding across the yard.

Jenny held Jess out to him and he took the puppy in surprisingly gentle hands.

'Now, Jess,' he said softly. 'What's happened to you?'

Jenny looked at the vet with surprise. Maybe he wasn't always noisy after all.

'That's a pity,' Tom said, as he looked at Jess's leg. 'I hate to see something like that.'

'Does that mean you can't do anything for him?' Jenny asked, her heart in her mouth.

'It depends,' the vet replied.

6

'First we'll take Jess inside where I can examine him properly,' Tom Palmer said.

Jenny followed the big vet inside, along with Matt and her father. Mr Palmer laid the puppy carefully on the kitchen table and began to examine him. 'How old is he? About four weeks?'

'Nearly five weeks,' Jenny replied. 'He's a bit small for his age because he had to be hand-reared.'

'Did you rear him yourself?' Tom asked. 'You've

done very well, lass. I'll have to try extra-hard with this little one.'

Jenny looked on anxiously, watching the vet run his hands over Jess's leg and shoulder.

At last, he looked up. 'I'll have to do some x-rays,' he said. 'But I'm pretty sure what the problem is: the shoulder joint on this front leg is out of line,' he explained. 'That's why the leg has grown at an awkward angle.'

'But can you do something for him?' Jenny asked hesitantly.

'Well, we might not be able to get his leg completely straight,' the vet told her. 'But I'm sure we can do *something*. The only thing is, he's not going to like it very much,' Tom warned her. 'I'll have to dislocate the joint and reset it. That way we can try and get the leg back into its normal position.'

Jenny swallowed. It *did* sound terrible. 'Will it hurt?' she asked.

Tom pursed his lips. 'I'll put Jess to sleep for the operation,' he said. 'He'll have to wear a cast for a while until the joint recovers. He won't like it, but he won't be in too much pain.'

Jenny swallowed. 'And it would be best for him in the end?'

Tom held Jess's twisted leg in his gentle fingers. 'I think so,' he said. 'But I can't make promises.'

'What do you think, Dad?' Jenny asked. 'Should we try? I mean, if it's going to be hard on Jess and then not work after all . . .' Her voice trailed off.

Fraser Miles looked serious. 'It's really up to you, Jenny,' he said. 'Jess is your dog. I only feel bad that I didn't send for Tom right away.'

Jenny put her arm through his. 'You let me keep him,' she said.

Fraser patted her hand. 'And as I said, he's your responsibility. What do you want to do – try Tom's treatment or leave Jess as he is?'

Jenny frowned. Mr Palmer had said that the treatment would be hard for Jess – maybe even painful. But the alternative was that Jess would never get any better than he was now. She found herself thinking of Jess of Beacon Brae. He would have taken the risk. If there was a chance of Jess having a more normal life, surely they should take the opportunity.

'Let's try it then,' Jenny decided. 'How long will it take before we know if he's all right?'

'A few weeks,' Tom Palmer replied. 'Of course,

when the cast comes off, his leg will be very weak. He'll need to exercise it. It'll be a lot of work for you.'

'I don't mind,' Jenny declared. 'I'll do anything if it makes him better.'

'Just remember,' said Tom, 'this may not work. And, even if it does, there's no guarantee that Jess's leg will be completely normal. It might always be weak. But I think it's worth a try.'

Jenny nodded. 'I understand,' she said, stroking Jess. The puppy looked up at her and licked her hand. 'Mr Palmer is going to do his best for you, Jess,' she whispered. 'His very best.'

'Oh, I'll do that all right,' said Tom Palmer, smiling down at Jenny. 'And I'll tell you another thing. I don't think Jess could have a better nurse than you, Jenny.'

Jenny looked up at him. 'Thank you,' she said. 'When will you do it?'

Tom frowned. 'I'd like to leave it until he's a little bit older – let's say three weeks from now. By that time he'll be stronger but his bones will still be soft enough to grow into a more normal position with the help of the cast. You go on doing what you're doing and he should be more than fit for the operation.'

'I will,' Jenny promised. 'I'll take *extra* special care of him.'

Matt laughed. 'You couldn't take more care of him than you are doing, Jen,' he said.

But Jenny had made up her mind. From now until Jess's operation the little puppy was going to come first every time. *Nothing* would be too much trouble.

Over the next three weeks Jenny read everything she could get her hands on about the rearing of puppies. Carrie Turner got interested too and together they made up a diet sheet for Jess. Carrie had started coming to tea once a week at Windy Hill. The first time she had seen Jess she had been completely hooked.

'Oh, he's gorgeous!' she said, stooping to pet the little puppy.'

'Come and see Nell's other puppies,' Jenny said, lifting Jess up. 'They're gorgeous too.'

'Aren't they allowed in the house?' asked Carrie as she followed Jenny into the stables.

Jenny shook her head. 'They're going to be working dogs,' she explained. 'They have to get used to it.'

'Poor little things,' said Carrie, bending down

to stroke the puppies. 'But at least they've got their mum.'

Nell looked up at them and Jenny gave her a pat. The puppies scrambled over each other, tumbling and playing. Jenny couldn't resist it. She put Jess in the box with them and watched as he began to make friends.

'He isn't really supposed to play with the other puppies,' she told Carrie. 'But he's managed to find his way into the stable several times. He can't see why they shouldn't all be friends.'

'They're much bigger than he is,' Carrie commented. 'But I still like Jess best.'

'Nell's puppies will be going to their new homes this afternoon,' Jenny said. 'Maybe it's just as well Jess wasn't allowed to play with them. He'd miss them when they went.'

'Oh, I don't know about that,' said Carrie, grinning. 'I can't see what harm being friends *ever* does. I mean you can't always be worrying about what's round the corner.'

Jenny grinned back. Carrie was so good to be with. She was showing Jenny a different way of looking at things. Jenny decided to stop worrying about Jess's operation and just enjoy him. After all, she was lucky to have the puppy at all!

★ ★ ★

'That's the last one,' Fraser Miles said later that afternoon. He tucked the fourth puppy into the big basket in the back of the jeep. 'Say goodbye now, Jenny.'

Jenny leaned over the basket with Jess in her arms. She stroked the puppies. Jess squirmed, eager to join the others but Jenny held him firmly. 'You're all going to lovely homes,' she said softly to his brothers and sisters.

'They are that,' said Mr Miles. 'There's been quite a bit of competition for Nell's pups. I got good prices for them. I reckon we'll see one or two of these at the sheepdog trials in Graston in a few years' time.'

'I'll take Jess to watch them,' Jenny announced, cuddling her pet.

Mr Miles smiled. 'I reckon Jess might sire a sheepdog or two in his time,' he said.

Jenny stared at him. 'Oh, Dad, do you really think so?'

Jenny's father looked at Jess. 'I don't see why not,' he said. 'After all he comes from good stock. Just because he can't be a working dog doesn't mean he can't sire good working animals.'

'Wow!' said Carrie as Mr Miles drove off with

the pups. 'Just imagine, Jen – a whole dynasty of champion sheepdogs all sired by Jess!'

'Protein and vitamins to help him grow strong and healthy,' Jenny announced to Mrs Grace on the morning of Jess's operation. 'And carbohydrates for energy – but not too many or he'll get fat.'

Ellen Grace laughed as she watched Jess scamper under the kitchen table. Jenny looked round the kitchen. Already it looked more like it had done when her mother had been alive. The jelly moulds were shining and Mrs Grace had run up new curtains from some material she had at home – red checks this time. She had also sorted out some different curtains and a pretty bedspread for Jenny's room. The flowered pattern looked much more grown-up than the old cartoon characters Jenny had had since she was tiny.

'Oh, Jess has got plenty of energy,' Mrs Grace said.

Jenny made a dive for Jess and scooped him up in her arms. The puppy was managing very well with only three good legs and he had grown amazingly. 'I hope you won't mind the cast too much, Jess,' she said, rubbing her cheek against his head. 'You won't be able to run about as easily with that on.'

'I'm sure he'll manage,' Mrs Grace put in. 'He's very brave. You'd better get off to school. You'll be late otherwise.'

Jenny gave Jess a final cuddle. 'Next time I see you your operation will be over, Jess. Oh, I hope it goes well.'

Jess looked up and licked her chin.

'Now, don't worry, Jenny,' Mrs Grace advised. 'Your dad will collect you from school and take you to the surgery to visit Jess.'

School, thought Jenny. How on earth was she to keep her mind on her schoolwork while Jess was having his operation? She wondered if Carrie would have any bright ideas about taking her mind off that!

'Why don't you get a decent schoolbag instead of that old thing?' Fiona McLay sneered at Jenny, as she arrived at the school gates.

'Jenny's schoolbag is OK,' said Paul, Fiona's seven-year-old brother. 'It's a *sports* bag.'

Jenny looked at Matt's battered old sports bag and smiled at Paul. Paul was deaf but he was a marvellous lip reader. Often people didn't even realise he was deaf – until Fiona told them.

'What do you know about anything?' Fiona snapped at him. She turned to Jenny. 'Well?'

Jenny was hardly listening. Jess would be on his way to the vet's about now and she couldn't think of anything else.

'Oh, I forgot,' Fiona said, looking down her nose at Jenny. Fiona was a lot taller than Jenny with short dark hair and ice-blue eyes. 'Your father can't afford to buy you decent things. When is he going to sell that old farm of yours? My dad says he can't last much longer – not with his money worries.'

Jenny looked at the other girl in frustration. Fiona always made her feel tongue-tied. 'I don't care what kind of schoolbag I have,' she said. 'And Windy Hill isn't for s-s-sale.'

'Oh, now you've got a stutter,' Fiona mocked. 'Windy Hill isn't for s-s-sale. We'll s-s-see about that.'

'Leave her alone,' said a voice behind Jenny.

Jenny whirled round. Carrie had just arrived. Her bright red hair was escaping from its ponytail and her green eyes were flashing. 'I'm fed up with you always getting at Jenny,' Carrie went on. 'You're just a bully. Why can't you pick on someone your own size? Can't you *see* she's worried?'

Fiona went bright red. 'She's worried about losing her tatty little farm,' she retorted nastily and she flounced off.

Little Paul looked embarrassed at his sister's behaviour and gave Jenny an apologetic smile. Jenny smiled back and looked at Carrie in admiration. Even the freckles across Carrie's nose seemed to glow with indignation as she watched Fiona storm off into the playground.

'I wish I could stand up to Fiona like that,' Jenny said. 'Thanks.'

'Don't mention it,' Carrie replied. 'I've been itching to give her a taste of her own medicine for ages. Anyway, how was Jess this morning? When will you know how the op went?'

'Dad's picking me up from school this afternoon to go straight to the vet's surgery,' Jenny replied. She saw Paul's face looking puzzled. 'It's my puppy,' she explained to him. 'He's having an operation today and I'm worried about him.'

'You're so lucky to have a puppy,' the little boy said. 'I wish I had a pet.'

'I haven't got a pet either, Paul,' said Carrie comfortingly.

'At least you can go to Puffin Island and watch the birds any time you want,' replied Paul. 'I love bird watching.'

'Do you?' asked Carrie. 'Then you should come for a trip to the bird reserve one day.'

'You mean in your dad's boat?' asked Paul excitedly.

Carrie nodded. Jenny knew that Mr Turner had a boat which he used to take people on trips to Puffin Island, just off the coast. The little island was a bird reserve and was home to nesting seabirds.

'You could come too, Jenny,' Carrie said. 'Mum wants to go out there anyway. She's got a commission to illustrate a book on birds and Puffin Island is perfect for it. We could *all* go.'

'Oh, I'd love to,' Jenny said. 'But shouldn't you ask your mum and dad, first? I wouldn't want to be in the way.'

Carrie put her head on one side. 'Typical Jenny!' she said. 'You're always putting yourself down.'

'Sorry,' said Jenny.

'See what I mean?' said Carrie, her hands on her hips.

They both laughed.

'You need someone to stand up for you,' Carrie decided.

'I'll stand up for you, Jenny,' Paul said. 'Fiona bullies me too.'

Jenny was shocked. How could Fiona bully her deaf little brother? That was really mean. Paul and Fiona were so different they didn't seem like brother and sister at all. Jenny could see Fiona crossing the playground towards them again. She suddenly felt sorry for Paul – not because he was deaf but because he had to put up with a sister like Fiona.

'How would you like to come and see Jess some day?' Jenny asked him.

Paul's face lit up. 'Can I really?' he said. 'I'd love that.'

Fiona came to stand beside Paul. 'No, you can't,' she said. 'You know Dad would never let you set foot on Windy Hill – at least not until we own it.'

Paul's face fell and Jenny felt a rush of sympathy for him.

'Well, I intend to visit Windy Hill as often as I like,' said Carrie.

'You!' said Fiona. 'What do you want to go visiting Jenny for?'

Carrie stuck her chin out. 'Because she's my friend,' she declared.

'Hmmph,' said Fiona. 'Your mum's a famous

artist. She wouldn't want you to waste your time on a nobody like Jenny Miles.'

'My mother would love Jenny,' Carrie retorted. 'In fact, she's invited Jenny to tea!' Carrie gave Jenny a look and Jenny blushed. She had been putting off going for tea at Carrie's, preferring to rush straight home to feed Jess. Maybe she should make time to visit Cliff House, the Turners' home in Cliffbay.

For the first time Fiona looked put out. Her face flushed an angry red and she grabbed Paul's hand. 'Come on, Paul. Dad wouldn't want us to waste our time talking to Jenny Miles.'

Jenny felt a hot surge of anger. Why should she always let Fiona get away with it? 'By the way, Fiona,' she said sharply, 'Windy Hill is *not* for sale – to your father or anybody else.'

Fiona looked as if she couldn't believe her ears, then she turned on her heel, dragging Paul after her. The little boy looked back as he went and gave her a weak smile. Jenny waved and smiled back.

'Wow!' said Carrie admiringly. 'Maybe you *can* stick up for yourself after all. Well done, Jenny!'

Jenny flushed. She felt elated, triumphant. She had stood up to Fiona McLay.

'I hope you didn't mind me saying that about coming to Windy Hill whenever I liked,' Carrie went on. 'I just got so *mad* at Fiona. She's always trying to wangle an invitation to Cliff House. She thinks Mum will want to paint a portrait of her. Some chance!'

'I didn't mind,' said Jenny. 'And, Carrie, I *will* come to tea. I promise – as soon as Jess gets home.'

'How about Saturday?' Carrie asked.

Jenny nodded. 'Saturday!' she agreed. 'And I'll bring Jess too, if I may.'

'I knew I'd talk you round,' said Carrie. 'Now, can you have a look at this maths homework of mine? I just don't know what algebra is *for*!'

Jenny shook her head. 'Sure,' she said. 'It'll take my mind off Jess.'

Talking to Carrie was a bit like dealing with a whirlwind but Jenny liked it. For the first time ever she had felt more important than Fiona McLay. Carrie had made her feel like that, by standing up for her and showing her how to stand up for herself. And, better than anything else, at last she had a friend!

7

Tom Palmer was smiling when he opened the door of the surgery to Jenny and her father.

'It went very well,' he said reassuringly. 'Jess is still a bit sleepy but come and see him. He's doing fine.'

Jenny's heart hammered as she followed Tom Palmer through reception and into the recovery room. Jess looked very small, lying in his cage. The cast on his leg seemed too big for the little puppy. Jenny touched it through the bars of the cage.

'It's lighter than it looks,' said Tom Palmer, guessing what she was thinking. 'It's a special plastic bandage called a vetcast. It isn't nearly as heavy as a plaster cast.'

Jenny moved closer to the cage and gazed down at Jess. The puppy's eyes were closed but when she said his name they opened slowly and his tail thumped against the bottom of the cage.

'Oh, Jess,' whispered Jenny. 'I was so worried about you.' She turned to Tom Palmer. 'Can I hold him?'

The vet nodded and opened the door of the cage, lifting Jess out carefully. He laid the puppy in Jenny's arms and Jenny bent her head and gave Jess a cuddle. Jess licked her cheek and his tail wagged harder.

Jenny touched the cast again. Mr Palmer was right. It wasn't so heavy after all.

'Will he have to lie still while he has the cast on?' Jenny asked anxiously.

'Not at all,' Tom Palmer assured her. 'He's so young he'll adapt to it very quickly.'

'It looks like you've done a good job there, Tom,' Fraser Miles said. 'What happens now?'

'I'll keep him in overnight just to make sure he's completely recovered from the anaesthetic,' the vet replied. 'You can come and collect him tomorrow.'

Jenny bent her head to Jess. 'Tomorrow, Jess,' she promised. 'You're coming home tomorrow and I'm going to take *such* good care of you.'

Tom Palmer was right. Jess soon got used to having the cast on his leg. Too used to it, Jenny thought, as she and Carrie watched the little puppy chase after Jake and Nell three weeks later.

The working dogs trotted across the yard, heads low and plumy tails waving. Jess limped behind the sheepdogs, yapping furiously but the older dogs took no notice.

'Keep Jess in the yard,' Fraser Miles warned Jenny as he opened the gate and the two sheepdogs followed him through. 'I don't want him anywhere near the sheep. He's a house dog and he has to learn to behave like one.'

Jenny hid a smile. Jess just couldn't help trying to follow Jake and Nell.

'It isn't Jess's fault,' Carrie whispered to her as Mr Miles whistled for the working dogs and set off up the track. 'Jess was bred from a long line of sheepdogs. It's in his blood.'

Jenny nodded. 'I know,' she said. 'But Dad is

right. He can't afford to risk Jess frightening the sheep or trying to play with Jake and Nell. It won't be long till lambing now and the ewes are easily upset when they're pregnant. Dad needs a good lambing. Everything depends on it.'

Carrie looked serious as she and Jenny walked back towards the house. 'Are things really that bad then?' she asked.

Jenny nodded her head. 'I think so. Dad doesn't talk about it. But Matt says if we don't get a good yield of lambs Dad will have to think about putting Windy Hill on the market.'

'And you know who'll be ready to buy it,' Carrie said.

'Fiona McLay's father,' Jenny replied, frowning. 'It would break Dad's heart to sell Windy Hill – and it would be even worse if he had to sell to Mr McLay. The trouble is, Fiona's dad seems determined to get our farm.'

'Why?' Carrie asked.

Jenny shook her head. 'Mrs Grace says he wants to buy up all the land round his farm. But I think it's to do with an argument they had years ago. I reckon Mr McLay still holds a grudge against Dad.'

'Well, I think you should concentrate on Jess

and forget about Mr McLay,' said Carrie. 'Come on, it's time for Jess's exercise.'

Jenny grinned as she followed Carrie into the kitchen porch. Carrie was always so full of enthusiasm. She had been a real help these last weeks.

'Just another week, Jess,' Jenny whispered to the puppy. 'Then we'll see what you can do without your cast.'

Jess looked up at her and gave a short bark. He was growing fast now. Jenny scooped her pet up into her arms. 'Now, where's your stick?'

Jenny found the stick behind the porch door and they took Jess out into the yard.

'It isn't very sophisticated, is it?' asked Carrie, looking at the stick.

'It works,' said Jenny. 'That's all that matters.'

Carrie looked at Jess as Jenny threw the stick. The puppy ran after it, sometimes forgetting to hold his bad leg out of the way in his excitement to fetch the stick. 'You're right,' Carrie said. 'Anything that makes him use that leg must be good for him.'

Matt came out of the house and stood watching for a while as the girls threw the stick for Jess. 'Why don't you try taking him down to the beach for a swim once his cast is off?' he suggested.

'Swimming?' said Jenny. 'Would that be good for him?'

'I've started taking Mercury down to the beach at Cliffbay,' Matt said. 'I gallop him along the edge of the water. That's really good for his legs. Maybe you should try it with Jess.'

'That sounds like a good idea,' Carrie said.

'Check it out with Tom Palmer,' Matt advised. 'But I don't see why it shouldn't work.'

Jenny watched as Matt went into the stable. A moment later he led Mercury out. The big horse looked sleek and well fed and he stood quietly while Matt saddled him. Jenny stared at Mercury. She was beginning to remember why her mother had loved the horse so much. He was *beautiful*.

He turned his head and looked at her, blowing softly through his nostrils. For a second, Jenny was tempted to move closer and touch the gleaming creature. But she couldn't. No matter how beautiful he was she still couldn't forgive him.

'The seawater certainly seems to have worked for Mercury,' Carrie said. 'What do you think, Jenny? Do you want to give it a go?'

Jenny didn't answer. She was still looking at

Mercury. Matt led the big black horse through the farm gate, mounted and rode off down the track. Jenny turned to Carrie and saw concern in her friend's eyes.

'You don't like Mercury, do you?' asked Carrie.

'No,' Jenny said quietly.

'But why?' Carrie asked.

'Because he killed my mother,' Jenny replied.

Carrie gasped in shock. 'What do you mean? How?'

'He threw her and she died,' Jenny explained. 'I just can't understand why Dad wants to keep him.'

'So why don't you ask him?' Carrie asked.

Jenny shook her head. 'I can't,' she said. 'Dad won't talk about Mum's accident.'

Carrie looked thoughtful. 'Your dad must have his reasons for keeping the horse,' she said.

'I suppose it's because he feels guilty that Mercury was so badly treated after he sold him,' said Jenny. 'It's the only reason I can think of.'

'Then why don't you tell Matt you're not happy about Mercury being here?' Carrie suggested.

'Because Matt loves Mercury,' Jenny said. 'Anybody can see that. I think he loves Mercury as much as I love Jess. Though I can't understand it.'

Carrie sighed. 'So what are you going to do then?' she asked.

Jenny shook her head. 'There isn't anything I *can* do,' she said. 'I've just got to accept it.'

Carrie was silent for a moment. 'What about Matt's idea of taking Jess swimming?' she said at last.

Jenny looked down at Jess. He was scampering round the farmyard, chasing a tuft of sheep's wool. Every time he caught up with it the breeze blew it away from him. Jenny felt better just watching him. She nodded. 'It's worth a try,' she said. Anything was worth a try if it helped Jess. But she would check with the vet first.

Mrs Grace came out of the kitchen into the yard. 'Tea's ready,' she announced. 'It's your favourite, Jenny — sausage casserole. Now leave some for your dad and be sure to put the dish back in the oven to keep warm after you've finished. I've got to dash into Greybridge to do some shopping.'

Jenny nodded. Mrs Grace had fitted in really well at Windy Hill and she was a terrific cook.

'Yummy!' said Carrie. 'I *love* sausage casserole. Come on, Jess, race you to the kitchen. That'll count as exercise.'

★ ★ ★

Carrie's mum drove up in her battered old Mini just as Jenny and Carrie were finishing tea. The two girls dashed outside to meet her. Jenny loved Mrs Turner's Mini. It was bright orange and she had painted big yellow sunflowers on the roof. Mrs Turner had had the Mini since she was an art student and refused to part with it, even though she could afford something smarter. Mrs Turner's hair was red like her daughter's but cut short. She looked as bright and cheerful as a sunflower herself. She and the Mini were a good match.

'How's the patient?' she asked as she got out of the car and caught sight of Jess.

'The cast is coming off next week,' Jenny replied.

Mrs Turner was studying Jess closely and looking very thoughtful. 'Next week,' she murmured. 'Mmm. Do you mind if I do a few sketches of Jess while he still has his cast on, Jenny?'

Jenny's mouth dropped open in surprise. 'Sketches! Oh, that would be great. But I don't know if he'll sit still.'

Carrie laughed. 'Don't worry about that,' she said. 'I've seen Mum chase animals all over her

93

studio while she's been sketching them.'

'Cats are worse than dogs,' Mrs Turner said, reaching into the back seat of the Mini. She brought out a sketch-pad and a box of pencils. 'Just put him down and I'll get on with it, Jenny. He's perfect.'

Jenny put Jess on the ground and the puppy began to chase his tail, falling over several times when he lost his balance. Carrie's mum perched herself on the bonnet of the Mini and began to sketch furiously. Her eyes flicked from Jess to the sketching block in front of her. It was clear to Jenny that she wasn't doing just one sketch. She was doing one after another.

As Jenny watched, Mrs Turner tore off the sheet she had been working on and tossed it on top of the bonnet behind her. Carrie made a dive and caught it as it slid off the car. Mrs Turner didn't even seem to notice.

'When Mum's hard at work the *sky* could fall in and she wouldn't notice,' Carrie explained, as another page slithered down the bonnet.

Jenny giggled. Jess was rolling round the yard now, trying to eat his cast. Mrs Turner's pencil was flying across the paper and Carrie was diving for pages as quickly as her mum tore them off and threw them behind her.

THE ARRIVAL

At last Mrs Turner stopped her frantic sketching and looked up. 'That should do to be going on with,' she announced. 'Thanks, Jenny.'

'Do you mean you might want to do more?' Jenny asked.

Mrs Turner grinned. 'I'll work some of these up and then I'll see if I need any more,' she replied.

'What for?' asked Carrie.

Mrs Turner's eyes twinkled. 'Just wait and see.'

She handed Jenny one of the pages. It had five or six thumbnail sketches of Jess on it. Jenny gasped with pleasure as she looked at the drawings. Though they were composed of only a few quick lines, Jenny thought they captured Jess's playfulness perfectly.

'Can I keep these?' she asked.

'Sure,' said Mrs Turner. 'Now, Carrie, let's get going.'

Carrie leaped into the car as her mother revved the engine.

Jenny grinned. Mrs Turner was amazing. Carrie has said her mother could sit for hours just looking at something she was painting, but when she moved, she moved *fast*!

Jenny looked again at the sketches as the Mini disappeared round the bend of the track in a cloud of dust. There was Jess sitting up, wide-eyed and innocent looking; Jess rolling on the cobbles, looking like an animated ball of black and white fluff; Jess chasing his tail, tumbling over his feet; Jess in all his moods – naughty, soulful, mischievous, adorable! The cast on his front leg made him even more appealing. Jenny turned to show the pictures to Jess but the puppy was nowhere to be seen.

'Jess!' she called in a panic. 'Where are you?'

There was a short bark from the kitchen and Jenny dashed inside. She stopped at the kitchen door, horrified. 'Oh, Jess!' she said. 'What have you done?'

But it was all too obvious what Jess had done. The casserole dish was still on the kitchen table. Jenny had forgotten to put it in the oven when she and Carrie had rushed outside to meet Mrs Turner. Jess stood over it, his tail wagging furiously. Somehow he must have managed to jump up on a chair and on to the table. He was licking his lips and the dish was wiped clean.

'You've eaten Dad's dinner,' said Jenny. 'What *is* he going to say?'

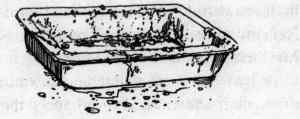

8

Jenny picked Jess up off the table and put him down firmly on the kitchen floor. 'Jess, that was really naughty,' she scolded, trying her hardest to sound severe.

Jess put his head on one side and looked up at her appealingly. Jenny couldn't help smiling as she took the empty casserole dish away from the table. 'At least there's nothing wrong with your appetite,' she joked. And, secretly, part of her was thrilled that Jess had ignored his weak leg in order to jump up to get the food. This must be a good sign! 'I suppose I'd better do something about Dad's dinner,' she said.

Jenny opened the larder door and scanned the contents. The larder was much better stocked since Mrs Grace had come to Windy Hill.

'Pasta,' Jenny decided, reaching down a packet of spaghetti. She frowned, then opened the fridge and considered the options. 'With cheese and tomato sauce,' she announced.

Jess wagged his tail and Jenny looked at him severely. 'Not for *you*, Jess. You've already had two dinners!'

Jenny unhooked an apron from the back of the kitchen door, put it on and set to work. By the time she heard her father arriving home the smell of the sauce was wafting through the kitchen and the pasta was ready.

Swiftly, Jenny drained the spaghetti and piled it into a serving dish. She poured the sauce over it, whipped off the apron and sat down in the corner armchair beside the Aga, cuddling Jess on her lap. 'Not a word!' she warned the little puppy.

Jess barked and licked a spot of sauce off her hand.

'Oops! Thanks, Jess,' she giggled.

Mr Miles came through the kitchen door, sniffing appreciatively. 'Hello, lass. Something smells good,' he said approvingly as he went to wash his hands.

Jenny set the serving dish in front of him at the table and watched anxiously as he helped himself.

'You know,' he said, taking a bite of his pasta. 'Mrs Grace really is a wonderful cook.'

Fraser Miles repeated his compliments next morning after breakfast.

'That pasta you left for me last night was delicious, Mrs Grace,' he said warmly.

Mrs Grace looked puzzled and she opened her mouth to say something. Jenny felt her heart sink. She looked quickly at Jess and away again. Then she saw Mrs Grace's eyes on her and felt herself blushing.

'I'm glad you enjoyed it, Fraser,' the housekeeper said solemnly. 'And don't you think it's time you called me Ellen?' she added, as Mr Miles made for the door.

'You've made quite a difference to Windy Hill since you've been here, Ellen,' he called back as he went out into the yard.

Jenny looked at the pots of spring bulbs on the

window ledge, the blue and white crockery gleaming on the dresser, the vase of bright yellow daffodils on the table. Mrs Grace certainly had made a difference – but would she be angry with Jess?

The housekeeper raised her eyebrows. 'Is there something I should know?' she asked, smiling.

Jenny couldn't help smiling back, and blurted out the whole story.

'I wondered if it might be something like that,' Mrs Grace said when she had finished.

'I thought you might be angry,' Jenny confessed.

Ellen Grace gathered up the plates from the kitchen table and dumped them in the sink. 'Angry?' she repeated. 'Not at all. It's nice to know that Jess likes my cooking too. But you might regret this episode, young lady.'

'Why?' asked Jenny, alarmed.

'Because now that I know you're such a good cook you won't be able to get out of helping me now and again.'

Jenny grinned. 'Oh, I'd love that,' she said. 'Thanks for not giving Jess away.'

Mrs Grace turned from the sink to look at her. 'That'll be our secret.'

Jenny smiled with relief. Mrs Grace was turning

out to be a very good addition to Windy Hill. 'You don't mind Jess being around, do you?' she asked. 'I mean he doesn't get in your way, does he?'

Mrs Grace laughed. 'He does,' she admitted. 'But I'm learning to put anything I don't want chewed out of *his* way! I didn't realise he could get up on to the table. I'll remember that in future. He'll be worse when he gets that cast off. Next week, isn't it?'

Jenny nodded. 'Mr Palmer is coming over after school on Wednesday to take it off. I hope everything will be OK. Carrie said she'd come over too if that's all right.'

'Of course it is,' replied Mrs Grace. 'It's good to see you've got a friend.'

Jenny opened the dresser drawer and started searching for something to tie her hair back with.

'Oh, I nearly forgot,' said Mrs Grace, wiping her hands on a towel. She went to her bag and brought out an elasticated hair-tie. It was yellow with blue splodgy flowers on it. 'This is for you.'

Jenny took the hair-tie and examined it. 'Thank you. I usually just tie it back with anything I can find,' she said.

Mrs Grace put her hands on her hips and gave

Jenny a look. 'I know,' she said. 'That's what comes of living in a house with no other women in it. This is much prettier. Now turn round and I'll fix it for you.'

Jenny did as she was told and Mrs Grace gathered her hair up and pulled it into a loose pony-tail. Then she twisted it up and fixed the hair-tie round it.

'There, what do you think of that?' she asked.

Jenny looked at herself in the dresser mirror, twisting round so that she could see the back of her head. 'Oh, that looks great, Mrs Grace,' she said. 'Carrie has a hair-tie just like this. What do you think, Jess?'

The puppy barked and wagged his tail.

'That looks like the seal of approval,' Mrs Grace said, laughing.

Jenny looked at her shyly. 'It was really good of you,' she said.

'Nonsense,' replied Mrs Grace briskly. 'I don't have any girls of my own to buy pretty things for. I've got a nephew but I can't buy hair-ties for him.'

Jenny giggled. 'I suppose not,' she said. 'What's he like?'

'You'll see soon enough,' Mrs Grace replied. 'He's coming for a long visit. His parents are going to Canada through his father's work and they need time to get settled down before they can send for him. They have to find somewhere to live and look at schools. It could take a while so he's coming to me for the time being. He'll be going to Graston School while he's here.'

'My grandparents live in Canada,' Jenny informed Mrs Grace. 'Grandad is Canadian. He came over here with the Canadian airforce. He was based at the old airfield on the other side of Greybridge. Then he met Gran and they got married. But he always said he would go back to Canada when he retired.'

'I remember your grandparents,' Ellen Grace said. 'I hope they're enjoying their retirement.'

'They love it,' Jenny enthused. 'They go camping and skiing and all kinds of things. Your nephew will have a great time in Canada. I'll show him some photos if you like.'

Jenny was about to ask more questions about Mrs Grace's nephew but she caught sight of the clock and jumped. 'Cripes! I'll be late for school if I don't hurry.' She gave Jess a quick cuddle and dashed out of the door. 'Try to be good, Jess,' she called over her shoulder.

'That'll be the day!' Mrs Grace called after her.

* ★ *

'There,' said Mr Palmer the following Wednesday. He stood back from the kitchen table. 'Let's see how he manages.'

Jenny and Carrie stood silently by as Jess looked up at the vet. The cast was lying on the table beside him and, for the first time in weeks, Jenny could see his leg. She drew in her breath.

'It looks straight,' she said.

Mr Palmer ran a hand over Jess's bad leg and the puppy wriggled. 'Not quite,' he said. 'I think he'll always have a bit of a limp, but what we're more concerned with is getting some strength into it.'

Jess licked furiously at his leg.

That'll be good for it,' Tom Palmer assured Jenny. 'Licking will stimulate the blood flow to the muscles. His leg muscles need building up.'

'Yes, it looks thinner than the other leg,' said Carrie sympathetically.

'That's only to be expected,' said Tom Palmer. 'You'll have to try and get him to exercise the leg.'

'We were going to ask you about swimming,' Jenny said. 'Do you think it would be good for him?'

'I think that's a brilliant idea,' the vet replied. 'Swimming would strengthen the muscles in his leg and, because he'll be suspended in the water, it won't put too much strain on him.'

Jenny picked Jess up gently. 'Do you hear that, Jess? You're going swimming. Won't that be fun?'

9

'Go get it, Jess!' Carrie shouted the following Sunday afternoon as she threw a stick into the sea.

Jenny laughed as Jess hurtled after the stick, splashing in the waves and throwing up sprays of seawater that sparkled in the sun. Jess was three months old now and well on his way to catching up on his growth. He was still a little small for his age but Tom Palmer had told Jenny not to worry about that. He would grow faster now that he was able to take regular exercise.

'He's certainly coming on,' said Mrs Turner, coming to stand beside Jenny.

Jenny nodded happily. 'The swimming is a great success,' she said. 'And he loves chasing sticks.'

Mrs Turner laughed as Jess raced up the beach and began to shake himself.

'Oh! I've had a shower already today,' Jenny cried, bending down to take the stick and fuss over Jess's cleverness. The puppy wagged his tail so hard he overbalanced and sat down suddenly on the sand.

'Still not entirely steady,' commented Mrs Turner, laughing.

'His right front leg is still pretty weak,' said Jenny.

'But you'd hardly notice he had a limp,' Carrie put in, running up to them. 'Oh, *look*!' She pointed to a sketch Mrs Turner was working on. 'He's still got his cast on.'

Jenny looked at the drawing. Mrs Turner was working up one of the sketches she had done of Jess. It looked very strange now that Jenny was getting used to Jess without his cast.

Mrs Turner held up the sketch and looked at it critically. 'I think I like this one best of all,' she said, examining her handiwork. The drawing showed Jess sitting, head on one side, looking up plaintively. The cast made him look very sweet and vulnerable.

Mrs Turner was lost in thought. 'Yes, I think this is the one I'll use,' she said softly.

'What for?' asked Carrie, plonking herself down on the sand beside Jess and rolling around with him.

Mrs Turner smiled. 'I don't want to say anything yet. If my idea works out I might have a very nice surprise for Jenny and Jess.'

Jenny longed to find out more but Mrs Turner shook her head. 'Time for tea,' she announced. 'Would you like to have tea with us, Jenny?'

Jenny had kept her promise to Carrie. Now she had tea at Cliff House as often as Carrie did at Windy Hill. This time Jenny shook her head. 'No, thank you. I'd love to, but I can't. Mrs Grace's nephew has arrived to stay with her for a while, and she's asked him to tea at Windy Hill today. I promised I'd be there.'

'What's he like?' asked Carrie, getting up and dusting sand from her clothes, as her mother walked on ahead.

Jenny shrugged. 'I haven't met him yet,' she replied. 'He only arrived last night.'

'Tea, Carrie,' Mrs Turner called from further along the beach. 'I've got a meeting of the Wildlife Association in an hour's time so we'll need to get a move on.'

Carrie grinned. 'Got to go. See you tomorrow,' she said, darting off.

'Come on, Jess,' Jenny called, picking up the stick. 'Let's go home.'

As they made their way along the beach towards the path at the far end of the cliffs, Jenny threw the stick as far as she could along the edge of the water. Jess scampered after it. Jenny watched him in delight. A wave caught the stick and drew it out to sea. Jess paddled after it, his legs working furiously as he swam. Matt was right. Swimming *was* good for Jess's leg.

Jenny watched as the puppy retrieved the stick and made his way back to shore, shaking himself and racing up the beach towards her. She took the stick and made to throw it again. Jess backed off, eyes alert.

'Oops! Sorry, Jess,' Jenny apologised as her aim went wide and the stick landed behind a rock at the base of the cliff.

Jess lolloped after it and disappeared behind the rock. Jenny waited but Jess did not reappear.

She frowned. 'Jess!' she called.

There was a muffled barking and Jess's head appeared round the side of the rock. He stood there, ignoring the stick, barking at her.

'What is it?' she called, walking over to him. 'Have you found a crab? Careful it doesn't nip you!'

Jess continued to stand there, legs stiff, barking urgently. Then he disappeared once more behind the rock.

Jenny began to run. 'What *is* it, Jess?' she cried. Then, as she reached the rock the breath caught in her throat. It wasn't a crab Jess had found. It was a sheep, lying motionless on the sand.

Jess stood over the sheep, barking furiously. But even without touching it, Jenny could see it was too late. The poor animal was dead.

Jenny looked up. The cliffs tumbled towards the beach in a mass of rock and scrubby grass. Shading her eyes from the sun, Jenny searched the top of the cliff. There was movement up there. More sheep.

Jenny's heart beat faster as she bent towards the dead sheep and examined it. It was a Blackface. The body was still warm and the blue marking on the sheep's fleece was visible. It looked like the

Windy Hill mark. Quickly she checked the tattoo on the inside of the animal's ear. It was one of her father's flock.

Jenny tried to picture the lie of the land above her. One of her father's fields was up there but it was fenced off from the cliff. Had some of the flock somehow broken through? Had somebody left a gate open?

As she looked up Jenny could see more movement. She listened and could hear the agitated bleating of frightened sheep. Jenny knew that if she didn't do something, more of her father's flock might panic and topple over the cliff. And it wasn't just the ewes that were in danger. Most of the flock was pregnant. If the ewes were lost, then their lambs would be lost too. Her father's whole livelihood was at risk.

Jenny looked at the cliff face. Was there any way she could climb it? Could she turn the sheep back? The cliff wasn't as sheer at this point as it was further along towards Cliffbay, but it was still steep. And there were loose rocks and stones that would make getting a foothold difficult. Jenny looked down at her trainers. They weren't the best footgear for climbing a cliff like that. But she knew she had no choice. It was either climb the cliff to try and turn the sheep, or watch as her father lost everything he had worked so hard for.

Jenny placed one foot on the side of the cliff. Jess looked up at her. 'I've got to do something, Jess,' she whispered, her throat dry. 'At least I've got to try.'

10

Jenny was a third of the way up the rocky slope before she realised that Jess was behind her. She turned, clutching at a spur of rock. 'Go back, Jess! It's too dangerous.'

But the little dog ignored her command and carried on up the cliff behind her, finding crevices and tufts of vegetation to give him footholds.

Jenny didn't know what she could do to stop him. What if he tumbled off and fell like that poor sheep down there? She opened her mouth to call to him but her handgrip slipped and she had to cling on to a tuft of grass to save herself from falling. One foot scrabbled at the surface beneath her as sand and gravel rolled away under her trainers.

At once there was a flurry of black and white and Jess was beside her, negotiating his own way up the cliff, testing, finding footholds. Jenny let out a sigh of relief as her foot found a grip, then she glanced at Jess. The little dog turned his head and looked at her, then began to scramble up the cliff in front of her.

Jenny let out a shaky breath of laughter. Jess was doing a lot better than she was. 'OK, Jess,' she admitted. 'You win. I'll follow you.'

Jenny was so intent on following where Jess led that at first she didn't hear the voice yelling from the top of the cliff. Then she became aware that somebody was shouting at her.

'Get back! What do you think you're doing? That cliff isn't safe.'

Jenny looked up, annoyed and ready to give as good as she got, but looking up made her dizzy. She gritted her teeth and kept on climbing. The voice above continued to shout.

'Nearly at the top, Jess,' she muttered as the cliff

face sloped inwards. Jenny leaned gratefully against the warm rock, clinging to it. Her nails were broken from scraping handholds. Her knees were scratched where the rock had grazed through her jeans.

'How stupid can you get?' came the voice.

Jenny looked up again, the sun dazzling her eyes. She could make out the shape of a boy, leaning over the cliff.

'Grab my hand,' he yelled.

Jenny reached up and grabbed the outstretched hand with her right one. Just as she did so the rock her foot was resting on rolled away from under her and crashed down to the beach below. 'Jess!' she cried.

The boy's other hand grabbed at Jess's collar and he hoisted the dog up on to the clifftop. 'Now grab that ledge,' he yelled, pointing at a narrow ledge near Jenny's left shoulder.

Jenny grasped the ledge, hauled on the boy's hand and heaved herself over the top of the cliff. She lay there for a moment, the breath rasping in her throat while the boy stood up.

'What on earth do you think you were doing?' he yelled. 'You could have killed yourself!'

Jess bared his teeth and growled at the boy. Jenny

had never seen him growl at anyone before. He was defending her.

Jenny looked at the boy. He looked about her own age. He stood up, towering over her, hands on hips. He had short brown hair and his green eyes were stormy with anger. 'The sheep,' she gasped, trying to get her breath back. 'I've got to turn them back.'

'And kill yourself while you're at it?' mocked the boy. 'People are more important than sheep.'

Jenny looked just beyond him to where the flock was huddled together, bleating pitifully. She took in the open field gate in the distance just as another of the sheep made towards the edge of the cliff.

The boy whirled and flapped his arms at the sheep. 'Get back!' he yelled.

Jenny scrambled to her feet. 'Don't!' she cried. 'You'll frighten them even more and then they'll all be over the cliff. Don't you know anything?'

The boy turned on her, furious. 'So what are *you* going to do about it?' he yelled.

But Jenny wasn't listening. Quick as a flash, Jess sped towards the straying sheep as it lumbered its way towards the cliff edge. The little dog crouched in front of the sheep, head low, eyes on the animal.

Then he darted forward, chivvying the ewe back out of harm's way.

'Jess,' Jenny breathed. She lifted her head and gave a low whistle. Jess's ears flattened and he sidled alongside the sheep, forcing it ever farther back.

Another animal broke from the flock. Jess scampered towards her, cutting off the sheep's progress and herding it back towards the rest.

Every time a sheep tried to break loose Jess crouched, eyes alert, head low, cutting off its route.

'Get round the other side of the flock,' Jenny ordered the boy. 'Make sure they don't break away. And *don't* raise your voice – *or* flap your arms! Can't you see they're nervous?'

Something in Jenny's voice must have told him she knew what she was talking about. He marched off, following her instructions to the letter.

Together girl, dog and boy edged the sheep away from danger towards the field gate. Now came the tricky bit – getting them safely back into the field. But Jenny needn't have worried. Sheep herding was bred into Jess's bones. The little collie was everywhere, nipping at the sheep's heels, weaving his way in and out of them, rounding them up, peeling off from the flock when one went astray to bring it back.

'Wow!' said the boy admiringly as the last of the sheep trotted through the gate. 'That dog is amazing. We've done it!'

Jenny closed the gate safely on the flock. 'That'll do, Jess,' she called, just as she had heard her father call many times to Jake and Nell after a job well done.

Jess came flying towards her and Jenny fussed over him, patting him and rubbing his ears. Jess licked Jenny's face, wagging his tail hard. 'If it hadn't been for you, Jess, those ewes would have been lost,' she said. Jess wagged his tail ecstatically. 'You'd make the best sheepdog ever, if it wasn't for your poor weak leg,' Jenny said, a little wistfully.

'I don't suppose *I* helped at all, did I?' the boy asked sarcastically. 'I mean *I* only saved you from falling down the cliff. But I suppose saving the sheep was more important!'

Jenny turned on him, all her pent-up anger breaking free. 'If they *are* safe it's no thanks to you, leaving the gate open. Don't you know how dangerous that is?'

The boy looked at her in astonishment. 'I *didn't* leave the gate open,' he protested. 'I was taking a walk along the clifftop when I came across these sheep all over the place. I was trying to *stop* them stampeding over the cliff.'

'By flapping your arms like a madman?' she snapped. 'That's the best way of frightening them.'

'How was *I* supposed to know that?' the boy retorted. 'I don't know anything about sheep. I was just doing my best.'

Jenny bit her lip. Maybe she had been a bit harsh on the boy, but she was so angry that someone had left that gate open. She frowned. Had someone left the gate open by accident – or had someone left it open on purpose?

She marched over to the track that bordered the field and looked at the ground. There were tyre marks. They looked quite fresh. 'Did you see anybody?' she asked the boy.

'No, I didn't,' he answered. 'And I'm getting fed up with you treating me like some kind of criminal. Anyway, how could anyone be stupid enough to risk their life for a flock of sheep?' the boy asked.

'You don't know the first thing about it,' Jenny snapped. 'Those are my father's sheep. They're ewes and they're pregnant. It wasn't just the flock that was in danger. It was all the unborn lambs as well.'

'And I suppose your father wouldn't mind you falling off the cliff so long as his sheep were saved,' the boy threw back at her. He looked at her stonily. 'You're off your head,' he said and turned and stomped off.

Jenny sighed. The boy had only been trying to help.

A wet tongue licked her hand and Jenny reached out and cuddled Jess to her. '*You* understand, Jess,' she said into the puppy's soft fur. '*You* know how important the sheep are.'

She looked up. The boy was fast disappearing along the clifftop.

Jess looked up at her, head cocked to one side. 'Come on, boy,' Jenny said, standing up. 'Let's get home and tell Dad about this. I've a feeling the gate being left open wasn't an accident at all.'

11

'You did well, lass,' Fraser Miles said, as Jenny finished her story.

'Jess did well too,' Jenny replied. She had washed and changed into fresh clothes. 'If it hadn't been for him we'd have lost some of the flock – maybe all of them. Perhaps he could help with the sheep now.'

Mr Miles ran a hand through his hair and smiled, his worried expression relaxing for a moment. 'Of course he did well,' he assured her.

'But you can't have a house dog working the sheep.'

Jenny bent and rubbed Jess's ears. 'I know that, really,' she agreed. 'But you *are* glad we kept him, aren't you?'

'Of course I am,' Fraser Miles said. 'But right now I want to find out what's going on. Where exactly did you see those tyre marks?'

Jenny told him and her father rose to his feet. 'We'd better go up there now, Matt,' he said to Jenny's brother. 'I'll get the jeep.'

Matt nodded and looked out of the window. 'We'll have to hurry. It's started to rain,' he said. 'Those tyre marks won't last long if we get a downpour. And we need to have a look at the ewes as well.'

'But the ewes are safe,' said Jenny.

'Look, Jen,' Matt said. ''Jess saved the ewes and that's wonderful, but they'll be upset and that could mean premature births. You know how much we're depending on them giving us a good yield this year. A bad lambing is the last thing we need.'

'Now, now, there's no need to worry about things before they happen,' Mrs Grace put in as the jeep's horn tooted from the farmyard. 'You get on up there with your dad, Matt. I'll have a cup of tea waiting for you when you get back.'

Matt grinned. 'That's your answer to everything, Ellen,' he said.

Mrs Grace laughed. 'I suppose it is,' she replied as Matt strode out into the farmyard.

Jenny watched as the jeep drove away.

'This boy you saw up on the cliff – what was he like?' Ellen Grace asked.

'Mmm?' Jenny murmured, gazing after the jeep. 'Oh, him. He was really rude and bad-tempered! Horrible!'

Just as Jenny finished speaking there was a sound at the door. 'Aunt Ellen,' said a voice. 'You'll never guess what happened.'

Jenny looked up and gasped as the boy from the cliff walked into the kitchen.

Jess growled, and the boy looked at him warily.

Jenny's mouth had dropped open. 'Oh, no! I don't believe it!' she burst out before she could stop herself.

The boy looked at her in dismay, his green eyes wide with surprise. 'You!' he exclaimed.

'This is Ian Amery, my nephew,' Mrs Grace said gently.

'But it can't be,' Jenny protested. 'He's the one I

was telling you about. He's the boy I had the argument with.'

'I thought it might be,' Mrs Grace replied. 'That's why I asked you what he was like.'

'And he's come for a *long* stay with you,' Jenny said mournfully.

'Don't worry. I'll be sure to stay well out of *your* way,' Ian retorted.

'You can start by going to get cleaned up,' Mrs Grace told him. 'You're nearly as dirty as Jenny was.'

Ian looked at his dirty hands. There were grass stains and streaks of mud on his jeans and sweatshirt. 'I was only trying to help,' he said, looking accusingly at Jenny.

'I'm sure Jenny understands that,' his aunt replied. 'And I'm sure she'll be very grateful when she thinks about it. The bathroom is that way.'

Ian trudged off and Jenny looked apologetically at Mrs Grace. 'Sorry,' she said. 'He's right. He *did* try to help.'

Ellen Grace smiled. 'I'm sure you two will be firm friends in no time,' she said confidently.

Jenny tried to feel as confident about that as Mrs Grace sounded, but, remembering the look Ian had given her when he came into the kitchen, she didn't think it was very likely.

By the time Ian had washed most of the mud off himself and his clothes Jenny had other things to think about. 'That's Dad and Matt,' she cried, hearing a car door slam.

Mrs Grace placed two mugs on the table as the two men came in. Jenny waited impatiently while the housekeeper introduced her nephew.

'I hear you saved Jenny from falling off the cliff,' Mr Miles said, looking intently at Ian. 'Thank you doesn't seem enough somehow.'

Ian blushed. 'I don't think she really would have fallen,' he protested. 'I just gave her a hand, that's all.'

Jenny danced with impatience. 'What about the *sheep*?' she asked. 'Are they all right? Did you find the tyre marks?'

Fraser Miles sat down at the table. 'The sheep seem OK but the rain had washed the tyre marks away. I'm pretty sure that it was Calum McLay but we'll never prove anything.'

'Calum McLay?' Jenny echoed. 'What makes you think that, Dad?'

'The tyre marks you described sounded like they were made by a Land Rover,' Matt said to her. 'Who else has a Land Rover round here?'

Mrs Grace sighed. 'And who else has a reason to do something like this?' she asked.

Jenny looked at them in dismay. 'Surely even *he* wouldn't do a terrible thing like that?'

'He might well be ruthless enough,' Fraser Miles replied. 'Calum McLay has wanted to take Windy Hill from me ever since I came here,' he explained. 'And now he is all the more determined. He wants to turn his own land over to forestry, but it won't be worth his while unless he buys up the rest of the land around here too – including Windy Hill.'

'Forestry!' Jenny burst out. 'But this is *sheep* country. He can't do that!'

Fraser smiled grimly. 'I suspect McLay might have more dirty tricks up his sleeve to get Windy Hill,' he concluded.

'What did you do to him all those years ago?' Matt asked his father. 'Beat him in a sheep-shearing competition? Walk off with the prize?' he joked.

Surprisingly, Fraser Miles smiled. 'A prize,' he mused. 'Something like that.'

Jenny wanted to ask more questions but Matt tipped his chair back and looked out of the window. 'We've got visitors,' he announced. A bright orange Mini drove through the gate.

'It's Carrie and her mum,' Jenny called, dashing outside.

Mrs Turner brought the Mini to a halt halfway across the farmyard and leaped out. Today she was wearing a bright pink shirt and purple leggings. 'I've got a surprise for you, Jenny,' she called.

Jess ran to meet her. The little dog's tail was wagging furiously. 'You'll wag that tail right off one day,' Mrs Turner laughed, bending down to pet him. Jess's tail wagged even harder. He loved Mrs Turner.

Carrie climbed out from the other side of the car as her mother dived into the boot and started to rummage about.

'Mum doesn't ever park the car,' she said to Jenny as they looked at the Mini skewed across the yard. 'It's more like she abandons it.'

'Come in out of the rain,' Mrs Grace called from the kitchen door.

'What's the surprise?' Jenny asked Carrie.

Carrie's face lit up. 'I can't tell you. Mum would *kill* me if I told you first,' she replied. 'But you'll love it.'

Mrs Grace was pouring water into the teapot. She set it down on the table and opened the oven door, drawing out a tray of hot, fluffy scones.

JESS THE BORDER COLLIE

'Oh, Mrs Grace, I could *die* for your scones,' Carrie moaned.

'There's no need to go that far, Carrie,' Mrs Grace told her, laughing.

'Here comes your mum,' said Jenny as Mrs Turner lurched across the farmyard, lugging an enormous folder tied with strings at one edge. Jess danced around her feet, threatening to trip her up as they both tried to get through the door together.

'Oops!' said Jenny, making a dive for the folder as Mrs Turner staggered into the kitchen. She caught it just in time and laid it down on the table.

'Thanks,' breathed Mrs Turner. 'Oh, Ellen, a cup of tea. Lovely!'

The folder was Mrs Turner's portfolio. Jenny knew that she used it to carry sketches and paintings to save them getting crushed.

'Have a look inside, Jenny,' Mrs Turner said.

Jenny undid the strings and opened the portfolio. She gasped at what she saw. There was Jess staring out at her. Not just quick sketches but a proper painting. Jess was looking straight at her, his head on one side. His leg was still in the cast and the look in his eyes was both pleading and friendly.

'Oh, Mrs Turner, it's beautiful,' Jenny breathed. Everyone else in the kitchen agreed.

Mrs Turner looked pleased. 'It's one of the best things I've done,' she said happily. 'But then, I had a very good model, didn't I, Jess?'

Jenny picked Jess up and showed him the painting. 'That's you, Jess,' she said softly. 'Aren't you just the most beautiful puppy in the world?'

'You aren't the only person to think so,' Mrs Turner said.

Jenny looked at her in surprise. 'What do you mean?'

Mrs Grace was leaning over the picture, admiring it. 'Something tells me this isn't the only surprise,' she said to Mrs Turner.

Pam Turner's eyes twinkled.

'Go *on*, Mum,' urged Carrie. 'Don't keep Jenny in suspense.'

'Jess is going to be famous – if you agree, of course,' Mrs Turner said.

'Famous?' asked Jenny, her eyes still on the painting. 'But how?'

'I was asked to do an illustration for an animal welfare fund-raising campaign,' Mrs Turner explained. 'I thought Jess was perfect for it – and so did the organisers.'

'You mean *Jess*'s picture will be used?' Jenny said, unable to believe her ears.

'Yes, on billboards, advertisements, leaflets – the lot,' Mrs Turner replied. 'The campaign organisers are really excited about it. They think Jess is just the image they're looking for. But I wouldn't be happy about letting them use my illustration unless you agreed, Jenny.'

'You said it was for animal welfare,' Jenny said. 'That means Jess will be helping other animals. Of *course* I agree. I'd be so proud of Jess.'

Mrs Turner smiled. 'I'm so glad,' she said. 'This campaign could really help animals that have been maltreated.'

Jenny thought of Mercury and the state he had been in when he first came to Windy Hill. Although she was still uncomfortable having the horse at the farm, she didn't like to think of other animals going through what he had gone through with his last owners.

'Jess and I would be proud to help,' she said. 'You're going to be famous, Jess!' she said, leaning down to hug her pet. Jess put his two front paws on her knees. Jenny stroked his bad leg. It seemed to be getting stronger every day. Soon, she hoped, it would be almost as strong as his others.

'The campaign organisers will pay a fee to use my illustration,' Mrs Turner went on. 'It won't be much, of course, because they're a charity, but I insist on sharing it with you, Jenny.'

Matt threw his head back and laughed. 'There you are, Dad,' he said. 'Jess is earning his keep after all.'

Fraser Miles smiled. 'After what he and Jenny did today they deserve a treat,' he said. 'What are you going to spend the money on, Jenny?'

Jenny put her head on one side thoughtfully. 'A proper dog basket for Jess to sleep in,' she announced. 'Instead of his old cardboard box!'

'Good idea,' said Fraser Miles.

Jenny was suddenly filled with happiness. She was surrounded by people she loved. For the first time since her mother had died the old kitchen was alive with voices and laughter. She thought how happy her mother would be to hear that laughter ringing round the kitchen again. The farmhouse looked much more like its old self.

There was only one difference – her mother wasn't there. Her mother would never be with them again. Some day Jenny would talk to her father seriously about her feelings. But right now she was happy to let herself bask in the warmth of the friendship that flooded the kitchen.

A small, wet tongue licked Jenny's hand. She looked down. Tears blurred her eyes for just a moment as she scooped Jess up and cuddled him to her. 'Oh, you would love Jess, Mum,' she whispered into his soft fur. 'You would just *love* him.'

h HODDER

Another Hodder Children's book

JESS THE BORDER COLLIE 2
The Challenge

Lucy Daniels

Jess the Border collie puppy owes his life to Jenny Miles, and he'd do anything for her. They're the best of friends and, together, they're ready for all sorts of adventures!

It's lambing season at the farm, and this year there are more orphaned lambs than ever. Without more help to feed them, there's a danger that many of the lambs will die.

Jenny sees how gentle Jess is with the tiny lambs – perhaps there's a way he can help . . . ?

Another Hodder Children's book

JESS THE BORDER COLLIE 3
The Runaway

Lucy Daniels

Jess the Border collie puppy owes his life to Jenny Miles, and he'd do anything for her. They're the best of friends and, together, they're ready for all sorts of adventures!

Jenny's friend Paul McLay has gone missing, and the whole village is out looking for him. Jenny has an idea where Paul might be found. But it's getting dark, and storm clouds are gathering. Jenny's rescue plan might help to save Paul, but will it lead her and Jess into danger?

ORDER FORM

Lucy Daniels

0 340 70438 1 JESS THE BORDER COLLIE 1: *THE ARRIVAL*   £3.99 ☐
0 340 70439 x JESS THE BORDER COLLIE 2: *THE CHALLENGE* £3.99 ☐
0 340 70440 3 JESS THE BORDER COLLIE 3: *THE RUNAWAY*   £3.99 ☐

All Hodder Children's books are available at your local bookshop, or can be ordered direct from the publisher. Just tick the titles you would like and complete the details below. Prices and availability are subject to change without prior notice.

Please enclose a cheque or postal order made payable to *Bookpoint Ltd*, and send to: Hodder Children's Books, 39 Milton Park, Abingdon, OXON OX14 4TD, UK.
Email Address: orders@bookpoint.co.uk

If you would prefer to pay by credit card, our call centre team would be delighted to take your order by telephone. Our direct line *01235 400414* (lines open 9.00 am–6.00 pm Monday to Saturday, 24 hour message answering service). Alternatively you can send a fax on *01235 400454*.

TITLE	FIRST NAME		SURNAME	

ADDRESS		
DAYTIME TEL:		POST CODE	

If you would prefer to pay by credit card, please complete:
Please debit my Visa/Access/Diner's Card/American Express (delete as applicable) card no:

Signature .... Expiry Date: ....

If you would NOT like to receive further information on our products please tick the box. ☐